Defining Her

A Novel

Samantha March

Defining Her

By Samantha March

Marching INK

This is a work of fiction. Names, characters, places and incidents are either the product of the author's imagination or are used fictitiously, and any resemblance to actual persons, living or dead, events, or locales is entirely coincidental.

Cover Design by Karan & Co. Author Solutions

Proofreading by EFC Services

DEFINING HER

To my readers. I am forever grateful.

Prologue

NELLIE

He blew on my nipple, lightly caressing the skin just below my belly button at the same time. I flinched, my eyes still closed.

"Not yet," I mumbled.

"Nells. Come on, Nellie. Baby, open your eyes. And your legs."

I finally did as he asked—well, with my eyes. I squinted at Calvin, lying naked next to me in bed. "What?" I harrumphed. "I'm exhausted."

"I need you." He positioned himself on top of me, grinning wickedly.

I finally eased my legs open for him, just like he knew I would. He knew me; he knew he was my weakness. Our sex had always been mind-blowing. Three, four times a day. Hours at a time on occasion. It really was spectacular what we could achieve together.

I felt him enter me and closed my eyes, finding our rhythm. Supremely satisfied, I let myself get lost in the moment.

* * *

Right at nine o'clock, Calvin and I strolled out to my Lexus IS 350, the black paint shining in the sun from a recent wash. He gave me a lingering kiss, left hand cupping my ass, right hand threaded through my hair. I rubbed against him, not ready to leave yet. Damn, what he did to me.

Finally, I pulled away. "I'll call you, okay?"

"Of course." He slid his tongue in one more time, then opened my car door. "Until we come again, beautiful Nells."

I winked and climbed in, fastening my seatbelt and starting up the vehicle. Once I was around the block, I exhaled, rolling my neck around in circles. Fuck, I was sore. Everywhere. Calvin was, let's say, large. XL. For a white guy, even. Trust me. I'd been with plenty of black men to know the stereotypes are true, but Calvin . . . he was right up there. And with him always making sure I was pleased first, I was sexually satisfied upon leaving his house.

I stopped at a red light, fumbling in my brand new Prada bag (a beautiful powder blue with gold hardware) for a piece of winter mint gum and my Anastasia Beverly Hills liquid lipstick. Veronica. Perfect. Bold, rosy, and beautiful with my dark hair and freshly spray tanned skin. I carefully applied it, flipping off the driver behind me who started honking when the light changed. You only got one shot when applying liquid lipsticks. No green light was going to fuck with my precise application.

Once finished, I peeled off, turning up Missy Elliott on my stereo. I loved driving alone. It was my quiet time, my jam time, and my beauty time, all wrapped into one. I rolled my window down. The air not as warm and humid as usual for August in Illinois. I wanted to enjoy it.

Entering the city limits of Oamark Park, I turned my music down to an acceptable level for the quiet suburban area I recently called home. I waved jovially to Mrs. Sandsy, who was walking down the street with her toddler, Morrison. I passed a group of teenage girls practicing a dance routine at Flora Park and little boys having batting and fielding practice, dreaming big of joining the Chicago Cubs (or White Sox) one day.

I pulled up to North Street, turning the radio to a light pop station as I approached the house. Entering the driveway of my 4000-square-foot, beautifully restored Victorian home, I did the final check before exiting the car. Oh yes, one more thing.

Reaching into the center console, I grabbed the light blue bag and pulled open the strings, dropping the jewelry into my open palm. Grabbing my purse, I slipped my engagement ring on moments before my soon-to-be husband, Harrison, greeted me in the driveway.

Chapter 1

NELLIE

Two Years Later

Monday morning. I always have a weird high come Monday morning. My alarm goes off at five but I'm usually checking the clock around 4:58 or so, ready to start my day. I have my schedule down. I get up, pull out my yoga pants and sports bra, and work out for an hour. Yoga, Pilates, Jillian Michaels, whatever I was in the mood for. I leaned toward Jillian on a Monday, because that bitch is no joke. She gets my blood pumping and the sweat dripping, and I love it.

Our gym on the first floor is pretty incredible. When we moved in here two years prior, just months before our big wedding, I was very specific in what I wanted, and a gym was a must. I loved working out. Yes, health benefits are great and everything, but slipping into size 2 skinny jeans and looking killer in a bodycon dress were simply necessities in my life. Not to mention keeping up with the Joneses in this neighborhood was a full-time job. Every housewife took a spin class or hot yoga session or had a trainer making house calls five days a week.

After my workout, I showered, then prepared a healthy breakfast. I preferred protein smoothies, fruit and veggie smoothies, a granola bar, fruit. You would never find me shoveling eggs and bacon and toast and sausage in my mouth the morning after a grueling workout. What the hell would be the point of that? Usually by the time I've finished eating, Harrison is up and moving around. Sometimes he would make himself breakfast at home, but usually he stopped by the coffee shop near his law firm for a to-go nosh instead.

I usually leave the house just before nine, which is what time the salon opens, and it's not far from our house. But this morning, I'm out the door and on my way to the tanning salon by eight o'clock. I always had an employee scheduled to open and prep the salon for the day, but I had to get out early that morning. Harrison had recently been able to do some of his work from home, so he didn't go into the office now until nearly ten o'clock. And I just couldn't sit at home with him and try to act normal after the text I received that morning.

I scampered off after dutifully kissing my husband on the lips and wishing him a good day at work. I own You Bronze, and I really am quite proud of it. Me—a business owner. Even though our location opened up nearly two years ago, I still sometimes get surprised, and yes, a thrill of pleasure, when I tell people what my career is. I might not be as important as my hotshot lawyer husband, but I employ people. I hand out paychecks every two weeks. I contribute to our community events and had the Chamber of Commerce do a ribbon-cutting ceremony when You Bronze first opened. And I help make people beautiful. Well, not that a tan solely made them beautiful, but everyone can benefit from a little bronze boost. A healthy glow was always better than the pasty, deathly looking white skin. And when we have winters like we always do in Illinois . . . well, a tanning bed and brown skin sure can boost your mood. It's been confirmed.

I pulled into the parking lot, grabbed my purse, and made my way inside after hearing the double beeps to confirm a locked vehicle. Not that I worried at all about this tiny suburb. Please. This area was about as *Full House* as you could get.

Kerri was wiping down the reception area when I walked in.

"Good morning, Nellie!" she greeted me with a megawatt smile.

I grinned back. "Morning, Kerri. What's shaking?"

"The weekend was totally killer! My bestie Carmen snagged VIP passes to Drink21 and we got bottle service all night. Hashtag hungover, all day yesterday!" She shook her head and kept on smiling. "What did you do?"

What did I do? Could I tell her a blast from the past that had a very real threat to my present had contacted me out of the blue? Probably not.

"Nothing quite as exciting as yours. Saturday, we did the 5K run in town, and Sunday, Harrison had to work at the office so I did some shopping and just had me time." Ah, the calm before the storm.

"That sounds nice," Kerri enthused, and I tried to stay in the moment with my employee, not letting my thoughts wander.

"How many spray tan appointments do we have scheduled today?" I asked, heading behind the desk and shaking the mouse, waking up the computer screen to pull up the schedule.

"Eight on the books. More than usual for a Monday."

"Well, Labor Day is coming up. Maybe all the housewives have big vacation plans that they need to be bronzed up for. Will you be good handling the morning by yourself until Kara comes in?"

"Of course."

Kerri was one of my best employees. Not only was she totally flexible on her hours, a good sales girl behind the desk, and kind of a clean freak, she also was certified to give spray tans. A huge bonus for business and we're the only salon in Oamark Park to offer that. You have to go into Chicago to find the next salon that does person-to-person spray tans. Kerri and Kara are the only ones in the salon that do the appointments and Kara only comes in on Mondays and Fridays, so we have to schedule those appointments out to accommodate everyone. We also have three Versa Spa machines, the ones where you step in and it sprays you four times in the front, four times in the back, and those machines have definitely paid for themselves. But the girls doing the spraying is where it's at.

"Thanks. I'll be in the office if you need me."

"Sounds good," Kerri singsonged as I walked away from the front area, opening the door to my office and setting my purse on the desk. I loved my office. I also had an office in our house, but this was where the magic happened. This is where I worked on schedules, paperwork, payroll, marketing ideas. This is where I could thrive. I always had to keep our home office in tip-top shape because we were constantly hosting events at the house, whether it be neighborhood dinners and wine tastings or business clients of Harrison. Because the office is on the first floor just off the kitchen, everyone would walk by it at some point in the night. I could never have a post-it sticking out, shoes on the carpet, or dishes by my MacBook. The decorations had to be perfectly in place, the picture frames nary a fleck of dust, and . . . it was robotic. No one lived like that. I don't know when we started living like that. It wasn't always that way.

My office at the salon was always a zoo. It was lived in, loved. I did . . . shit here. I got shit done here. I owned a business in here. Not having paperwork strewn all over the place? Not happening. The only reason I didn't have dust in my office was because Kerri often took her cleaning prowess in here from time to time, tidying up for me (which I promptly mussed up) and dusting the computer screen and pictures frames and mopping the floor. Bless her.

I pulled up the schedule and minimized it to a small square, dragging it up to the top of my screen. I loved keeping an eye on the appointments, seeing the client name turn purple upon checking in, then yellow when their room was cleaned after they were finished. Our salon had three Versa Spas and sixteen regular tanning beds, all varying in speed and power. Mondays could be a fairly busy day, as people have their high hopes for the week, their mental to-do lists of how to get it started off right. Even during summer season the tanning salon stayed busy. Heaven forbid one of the suburbanites looked less than stellar taking their children to the pool or their summer activities and camps.

I blew out a breath. I could feel my old self threatening to peek through my carefully worked on new persona. My Mrs. Hawthorne persona. I wasn't the old Nellie. I wasn't.

I turned back to the computer, watching the check-ins and check-outs start to happen. I scanned the schedule again. Mostly familiar names in there. One in particular stood out to me on that day. Prue.

I clicked on her profile, which opened up the client information, including their photo we scanned from their driver's license. Yep, it was the woman I'd been observing the past . . . oh, two weeks or so. Cute blonde bob, though longer now than in her picture. Bright green eyes. Petite. I remember being the one to give her the tour when she first joined as a member. I towered over her, and I'm 5'7".

She stuck out to me because she seemed so . . . sad. Something in her piercing green eyes stuck out to me that day. I didn't know what her story was and I knew it wasn't my business. We all deal with our own shit in our own way. But something . . . just gave me a pause. I never really had an empathic bone in my body, and I wasn't the girlfriend type. I tried doing that whole have chicks on my side that I can count on and have each other's backs years ago and that didn't pan out. Nah. It's just me and Harrison now. And our neighbors and Harrison's work friends and the girls at the salon, but these are all acquaintances or employees. Not friends.

Working on a graphic for the Labor Day sale distracted me from my thoughts, and I forgot about Prue and much of anything else. I worked on a color scheme that popped, a layout that was aesthetically pleasing, and squeezing in all the pertinent details to the sale. At noon on the dot, my phone gave a chime. Time to break for lunch. If I didn't schedule my reminders, I would forget to eat all together. And yes, I cared about my body and my health and I worked out, but I did not skip meals. I was not anorexic or bulimic, thank you so much. I was healthy.

I drove to the deli and picked up a typical lunch—turkey and cheese on wheat bread, loaded with spinach, green peppers, lettuce, a few pickles, and low-fat Italian. I asked for an apple and, back in the office, grabbed a Smart Water out of my personal mini fridge. I watched YouTube videos while I ate—everything from how to perfect my winged liner to design tips to music videos. This was my time to zone out. To forget work and deadlines and schedules and invoices and just chill.

At ten to one, I started cleaning up my mess. Throwing my wrappers away. Wiping up some apple juice dribbled next to my MacBook. Clicking out of YouTube and getting back to the daily schedule. And, just like clockwork, I watched Prue's name become highlighted. She tanned Monday and Thursday at one o'clock each day. Ten minutes a time, though she stayed in the room for nearly twenty.

I headed out to the front desk, while Kerri took off for the day. The next employee, Sasha, was scheduled at two o'clock, so during this hour, I sat out front and checked people in and out and cleaned rooms. I loved my job. My career. My business. And while no, I didn't need the salon to help us financially, I loved having a schedule. A normalcy to a life that had rarely seen any. A purpose.

"Have a good rest of your day, Kerri. I'll see you in the morning."

"Sure thing, Nellie. Catch you on the flip." Kerri waved enthusiastically and headed out the door, gaudy pink Coach purse slung over her shoulder, already thumbing away on her ginormous cell phone. I made a mental note to buy my best and favorite employee a *real* designer purse this year as her Christmas bonus. Coach was so . . . basic.

I shook my head as I took a seat behind the reception desk. Listen to me! Coach was basic. How so much could change in so little time. If you had told me this would be my life at twenty-nine not even ten years ago, I would have laughed in your face. Or tried to rob you.

I looked up when I heard a noise and saw Prue approaching the desk, head down, car keys in hand.

"Thanks for coming in!" I said cheerily, a smile on my face.

She glanced back at me, just for a moment, but I saw the tears slipping down her face before she managed to put her sunglasses on. "Thanks," she practically whispered, before she was gone.

I frowned, looking at the screen. I checked out her room on the computer, then proceeded back to room 8 to give it a clean. Wiping down the bed, I couldn't stop thinking about this particular client. Why was she giving me the vibe that I should . . . help her? Offer her a shoulder to cry on or at least just someone to talk to? Maybe she was like me and never had a real friend she could count on. Maybe I could be that person for someone. Maybe making a new friend was just what I needed right now. To remind me that I had changed my life for the better, and I could still be that better person. Maybe the timing was perfect, what with my past threatening to return. This was the life I ran away to. I had to keep it together.

I placed new towels on the bench and exited the room. Next time I saw Prue, I would ask if she would like to grab coffee. Today was the third time I saw her crying while leaving. I was the owner of the salon. I needed to be friendly with my clients. She was clearly using my store for some sort of personal therapy session. I could reach out to her, solely as a business owner showing empathy for a client, and try to help. Maybe it could actually help me in the long run. She probably had more sincere problems than the women in my neighborhood.

"Ivander had a cold last week and the nanny insisted on basically abandoning the other children to be at his beck and call. I mean, he has his own iPhone. I told him to text her when he needed something, but no. Kimchi and Magdalena said they had to order in lunch every day last week because she insisted on being focused on Ivander. I mean, the girls are only sixteen! They shouldn't have a burden like that just because their brother is sick."

That was Anne, who was like Basic Barbie that tried too hard not to be basic. She hid her plain features—straight brown hair, boring brown eyes, average chest—by wearing too much makeup, wigs, and push-up bras that shouldn't be seen on an almost-forty mom of three. And I think she tried to make up for her average name by naming her children the most outlandish and foreign names she could. I felt bad for her husband, the friendly Gus who did our taxes. Sure, he was a pretty boring accountant, but he was a nice guy.

"Matt said he was going to a friend's house yesterday, so I casually drove by the friend's house just to be sure his bike was there. It was. And then Clara said she wanted to go the mall to meet with her friends, so after I dropped her off I went inside myself, just to make sure she was meeting her friends and not some pedophile on the Internet. She was. But I'm a mother. I can never be too sure my kids are telling the truth and staying out of trouble."

Jeanie was our resident helicopter mom. Her kids couldn't breathe without her watching and approving. She followed—no, stalked—them all over town. She chaperoned everything she could—including Matt's prom. I felt bad for the kids.

"Our sauna broke down last week. The repair man said he can't come for four days. Four days! I use that sauna twice a day. I need my sauna. Can you believe the audacity? If my skin suffers from this . . ." Another childless neighbor like me, Sophia always complained about how rough her life was. Because her in-house twenty-person sauna broke down, or her favorite massage therapist was out on maternity leave, or her husband bought her the wrong shade of yellow in the latest Gucci purse at Christmas. I swear, I preferred to listen to the mothers' problems over those without children. At least they had some depth. These women clearly had no idea what a rough life actually consisted of.

As I made my way back to the desk, ready to continue on with my day, I made the decision to approach Prue next time I saw her crying in my salon. As a professional courtesy.

Chapter 2

PRUE

My phone started ringing promptly at 7:30. I rolled over and groaned, reaching out with my right hand to grab it, as Clemmie was lying on my left. I squinted with one eye, just to make sure I saw the familiar name on my screen. Who else would be calling me at 7:30 on a Monday morning except, of course . . .

"Hello, Mother."

"Prue, darling, how are you this morning?"

"Still in bed. Like a normal person."

"It's nearly eight o'clock," she rebutted.

"I don't have a depo scheduled today."

"Oh, good. That's actually why I was calling."

I inwardly groaned. Of course. "Mom, why don't you just give me a regular schedule? Then I can actually plan my days around helping you."

"We plan to hire someone here at any moment and we will no longer need your wonderful services. But it would be a big help, honey, if you could be here by 10:30."

"Okay, okay. I'll be there."

"Love you, sweets. See you soon!"

Mom was chipper as she got off the phone, and I wanted to fling it across the room. But of course, I didn't. I set it gently back on the nightstand, wriggled my arm out from under my faithful yellow Lab, and rubbed the sleep out of my eyes. Darn it. My flipping day off. But I knew. Mom called me faithfully on Monday, Thursday, and Friday to help out at her school. Last night when I went to bed at the respectful time of 10:30, I knew Mom would call me bright and early. I just didn't want to admit it.

"Come on, girl. Let's start our day," I whispered to Clem. She stretched deeply, opening her mouth wide to show me all her teeth. Licking my face, she looked at me like I was her best friend. Because I was. A girl and her dog. Could there be a better bond?

I got out of bed first, shuffling to the bathroom to pee, brush my teeth, and wash my face. I decided to skip my moisturizer when I heard Clemmie give a whine. She was already lying by the closed bedroom door, and gave me a longing look when I peeked out to check on her.

"I'm sorry, girl. Do you need to go potty? Let's go, babe!" We hustled down the hallway and I unlocked both locks on my patio door and pushed it open, letting Clemmie go do her thing in the tiny patch of grass I had outside my deck. Apartment living was not for dog owners, as I was reminded daily. Poor Clemmie knew a big beautiful yard as just a young pup, and then it was ripped away from her when I was forced to move here. But I would have a house again soon. I knew it. I just needed a little more time to recover, let my credit score recover, and mentally move on.

After I let Clem back in, I quickly checked my email and then tried my hardest not to get sucked into social media while making myself breakfast. Scrambled eggs, toast, grapes. Orange juice. Mmm. Breakfast. I mixed in some eggs with Clemmie's breakfast, and she greedily wolfed it all down.

After, I threw my dishes in the sink and strapped on Clemmie's harness and slipped on my tennis shoes. Out for our morning walk. I enjoyed the feel of sunshine on my face, knowing that it wouldn't be too much longer before the fall came then . . . Illinois winter. While I loved winter and snowfall, sometimes it could be a little too much, even for me.

I walked through the quiet streets of Oamark Park. I missed the hustle and bustle of living in Chicago. Riding the train every day. Walking through the streets while eating a sandwich. Popping into the shops on the Magnificent Mile, most times just to browse. This was quite the change of pace.

Clemmie tugged on the leash as she went to inspect a grasshopper on the sidewalk. She sniffed at it a few times, then lost interest and kept moving along. We set up a solid pace, my Fitbit logging the miles and the calories I was burning. That hearty breakfast would be forgotten after this four-mile walk.

Once back home, I had just over an hour to get showered and changed and to the school. My mom, Jean

Doherty, was the principal of Eakwood Elementary School, one of the three elementary schools in this small town. School had only been in session for two weeks but I found myself there three days a week helping out. They got unexpectedly short-staffed in several places right before the school bell rang for the first time, so I was filling in. Because I didn't have anything else going on in my life. Right.

I was a court reporter and worked hard at my job. But it wasn't your typical 9-5 desk job. Some days I worked in the courtroom from eight in the morning to two in the afternoon without a break. Some days I worked solely from home, transcribing notes and proofreading the depo. Not very often would you find me in the office of my employer, Swank and Marty, because it simply wasn't needed and now it was too far to travel. Just three blocks west of Michigan Avenue, when I lived in Chicago I was there much more often, simply because I enjoyed being there and around my co-workers. That changed real quick when I learned one of my office-friends, Brandi, was sleeping with my boyfriend. That put a real damper on the office morale, especially when I learned she moved into the house with him that I cosigned my name to on the mortgage. Yeah. That stung.

After my relationship imploded, I hightailed it out of Chicago and to Oamark Park, to be closer to my mom. Since my dad died three years prior and I was their sole offspring, I often wanted to be closer to her. It was only about an hour drive from here to Chicago and I came back nearly every weekend to be by her or bring her into Chicago, but it was different being just minutes away from each other now. And being that I was at her school so much, we saw each other on nearly a daily basis. I wasn't complaining because I loved my mom and our relationship was fantastic. I just didn't . . . expect life to turn out this way.

It was all planned out. I had been with Deacon Moore for three years. We were in love. We met through mutual friends at a birthday party one night and had our first date just days later at Portillo's. He was everything to me. My best friend. My biggest supporter. He gave me shoulder rubs when I was hunched over my steno machine all day and night. He brought me foot-long sandwiches when I was in the courtroom and only given a ten-minute lunch break. He eventually started working in my office, which I loved. He came home with me and charmed my mother. I thought a proposal was coming anytime. We bought a house together. It was my own version of a fairy tale.

Until it all came crashing down. Turned out the perfect Deacon wasn't quite as perfect as I thought he was. He had been seeing Brandi on the side for nearly eight months. Eight months. We signed the mortgage papers as he was sleeping with another woman. How . . . how could someone do that to a person? And why? Why make me waste so much time and money and energy when he didn't even want to be with me? What was the point?

Though money was never really much of a concern for me—Dad had a good life insurance policy and court reporters made a better-than-decent salary—but Deacon was still slowly draining my finances. I paid for the home inspection, the realtor fees, the upfront taxes. I paid the loan payments on the new car "we" purchased together but only Deacon still drove. Deacon and Brandi had missed three mortgage payments and the bank called me to get that paid because my name was still on the mortgage. All that nonsense has led us to court, which means . . . more money being drained out of my account. I couldn't believe I made such a mistake. That I was so easily fooled. That I was betrayed by my lover, my best friend. Betrayed by a co-worker and someone who I was at least friendly with, if not real friends. And the fact that it totally upended my life was just the cherry on top.

I went from thinking a marriage proposal was on the way, moving into a beautiful home, bringing a new puppy into our lives to living in a small cramped apartment with my finances in jeopardy. Suing my ex-boyfriend and his new girlfriend to try to gain back some of the money that I spent paying their freaking mortgage. It just wasn't fair.

I pulled up to the school and parked in the employee parking lot. Walking in, my thoughts were still on how my life turned so quickly. What did I do to deserve such deceit? I was the good girl, the good person. I had morals and always tried doing the right thing. Karma scared the crap out of me. I was the dependable, reliable one. How was this fair, karma? Huh? It wasn't. It just simply wasn't. And that infuriated me. What was the point of always making the right choices if this is what I got in the end?

I trudged inside, barely noticing the sunshine on my face. My thoughts were dark, and I rarely let them go there. It was exhausting always trying to do the right thing, be as unselfish as I could be. Always putting others first, myself second. It wasn't fair to me. Maybe I needed to make some big changes in my life.

"Miss Prue!" All of a sudden, a little missile in a lime-green shirt flung himself at my legs.

"Hi, Lucas!" I patted the third grader on the back, my thoughts immediately dissolving and getting into school-mode.

"Are you in the lunch room today?"

"Sure am, dude. And the library!"

"Sweet! See you there. Peace out!"

I gave a wave as he continued walking down the hallway with his class as they headed toward the double doors leading out to the playground.

I walked into the office, waving to Margie behind the desk. She was the school secretary, had been here for nearly as long as my mom had been. I knew her well as she was also one of Mom's closest friends and considered her to be like a pseudo-aunt to me.

She was on the phone, so she just gave me a wave, and I took a left and entered Mom's office. She was behind her desk, typing on her laptop. "Hi, honey," she said as I entered, taking off her glasses and setting them on her immaculate wooden desk. Mom was one of those that never had clutter, never a paper out of place. Her OCD about cleanliness had definitely rubbed off on me. Not that I was mad about it.

"Hi, Mom. How's the morning been?" I asked, pulling open one of her bottom drawers and setting my small purse inside.

"Busy as usual for a Monday. I'm just putting together some ideas for a fun run we're going to do for the fourth grade class."

I dropped into the chair, grabbing my name tag that

Mom had set out for me on her desk and swinging the lanyard over my neck.

"What was that one again?" I asked.

"We're having the fourth grade class raise money for their mile run. It's the same idea as like a 5K charity run, except the class will just run a mile around the school on Friday, September 6. All the money raised will come to the school and be used to buy iPads, equipment, et cetera. I'm going to do the run with them, as well as all the fourth grade teachers, too. The parents will get to come and cheer them on, and then afterwards we're going to have a picnic in the park that will be catered donation-style from Friars Pizza."

"That sounds incredible, Mom. I bet they will have so much fun."

"I think so, too. How was your weekend?" She peered at me, like she was trying to read my thoughts before I spoke them aloud.

I shrugged. "Fine. Nothing much to report." That might not have been totally true after the strange occurrence I had on Saturday morning and then again on Sunday morning, but I couldn't talk to my mom about that yet. Who knows what I could even say? Maybe I met a guy but I don't know yet? That sounded stupid.

"Are you sure?" Mom's voice was gentle. Always treating me like the only child I was. So delicate.

"Yep. Anywho, lunch and library today? Anything else you need?" I changed the subject quickly.

"Yes. All six lunches if you can. No recess today. I pulled Ben for double duty instead. Then library for two classes after fifth grade lunch. You'll have the first and third graders. Sound okay?"

"Sounds great."

"Are you busy with work today?"

I shrugged. "Nothing terrible. Need to transcribe when I get home, and then I have to be in court starting at eight a.m. tomorrow. I heard from our secretary to be prepared for a long day."

"Do you want to come in Thursday or do you think you'll need a break?"

"No, I can make it. It's not a problem." I didn't want to leave Mom in a lurch. I just hoped I could get some decent sleep Wednesday night.

"Okay, dear. Well, head on off to the lunch room. Walkie me if you need help with the fourth graders."

"Will do. Have a good day, Mom."

I left the principal's office and walked to the lunchroom. The fourth graders were the most notorious class we had at Eakwood Elementary School. They were loud, seemed to forget all manners when entering the lunch room, and talked back. I dreaded when I watched these kids trickle in, knowing I had to be stern when it came to their class. That just wasn't my personality. I much preferred the kindergarteners, who just needed help opening all of their lunch items—from juice boxes to apple sauces to plastic containers—and wanted to tell me about their night and their pets and their moms. They were so sweet.

I entered the lunch room and waved to the gals behind the serving counter, preparing today's meal of French toast sticks. Oh goodie. Syrup day. I always left a sticky mess after days we served syrup. I walked over to

Maisy, the other lunchroom worker. She was in her upper thirties and had a daughter in the first grade class and son in the fifth grade class. Also two in high school, freshman twin girls. She was happily married and still talked about having another child, which blew my mind. Four kids, including a set of twins just entering high school, and she wanted another? But she was the definition of a suburban mom. She worked each year at a school in some capacity, and this year it was lunchroom/recess duty at Eakwood Elementary to be close to her two youngest children. Last year she was the eighth grade cheer volunteer mom when both her daughters were in the program, and the year before that she coordinated the KinderCare program here as well. She was very friendly and bubbly and waved eagerly at me when I walked in.

"Hi, Prue! How are you this morning?" she asked, her Barbie-blue eyes sparkling.

"Morning, Maisy. Pretty good so far. How about yourself? Did you have a good weekend?"

She launched into a play-by-play of their weekend festivities, which all revolved around the children. Their sports, activities, play dates, a birthday party. Pedicures with the twins to celebrate them making it through the first two weeks of high school. I nodded politely while scanning over the food options, making sure I knew what I had to tell kids to take. Looked liked grapes today. Good. Kids liked grapes.

The first class, second graders, started trickling in and Maisy and I took our usual stations—me by the sides line to make sure kids were getting their full meal per Michelle Obama (at least a full serving of either the fruit or vegetable offered, otherwise their hot lunch wouldn't count) and Maisy on seating duty. There were very strict rules about separating hot lunch and cold lunch students, because of the dreaded peanut allergy, something that sure wasn't around when I was in elementary school.

As my work day at school officially started, I forced all thoughts of Deacon, Brandi, and bills out of my mind. Time to focus on these kids . . . and think about the next time I could walk Clemmie and hope to bump into Hot Running Guy again.

NELLIE

15 Years Ago

"Mom! You forgot to pick me up again!" I stormed into our house, my book bag bouncing off my back. "Mom?" I yelled, not seeing her in the kitchen or the living room or the bathroom. Our apartment was so tiny those rooms were basically just one big room, but I stormed through them quickly and into her bedroom. Mom was lying on the bed, on her back.

"Mom!" I went over to her in a huff and shook her. Slowly, she blinked her eyes open.

"Whaaaa? Saaa matter, baaaaby?" she slurred, only opening one eye. I noticed bruising around her right eye and more purple marks just below her left temple. Anger flared through me.

"Where were you? I waited outside school for an hour before I just walked home. I fucking walked, Mom! Do you know how long that took me?"

She opened both eyes now, squinting at me. She cleared her throat. "Don't use that language around me, you ungrateful brat." Somehow, her words sounded much better than just moments ago. "I didn't know I was supposed to pick you up today."

I rolled my eyes. "You're supposed to pick me up every day. I go to school every day, Mom. Nothing about that has changed."

"Not on the weekends. I thought it was Sunday," she tried to protest, closing her eyes again. She reached over and grabbed a pillow, hugging it to her middle. I saw the

29

marks on her arms then.

"Did you forget about me because you're using again? Do you want me to get fucking taken away, Mom? Do you?" I was practically screaming.

"Lower your fucking voice, missy. Do you want the cops to come again and take you away? Huh? Is that what you want?"

I turned away in disgust, feeling the tears in my eyes. "Maybe I do," I mumbled under my breath.

"What did you say?"

"What the fuck ever, *Mother*. I'm going out."

"Where do you think you're going?" she shouted after me.

"Like you give a flying fuck!" I yelled back, putting a few items in my book bag and heading back out the door. Mom would simply fall asleep again for a few hours, then wake up and attempt to make dinner—either by going downstairs and hitting on the single old dude and convincing him to eat pizza with us and making him order it, or putting mac 'n cheese on the stove and calling it a night.

I headed to Billy's house. His parents were both doctors and were always gone all night. His housekeeper would make us a real meal so I wouldn't have to dine and dash at a restaurant that night. I had been doing it so much lately that I was worried about getting caught. I was running out of places to go and feared being recognized.

Billy opened the door, his hair damp from a shower. "Hey, Eleanor. What's up?"

I shrugged. "Doing anything tonight? I thought we could hang for a while."

"Sure. Come on in." He opened the door wider for me, and I stepped into the foyer. "Did you walk here? You look . . . winded."

I snorted. "My mom apparently thought it was Sunday and napped instead of picking me up, so I walked home and then pretty much straight here."

I followed Billy as we walked through his house—mansion—and he poked his head in one of the first-floor bathrooms where Lolita, the housekeeper, was coming out of. "Hey, Lo, can you cook up enough for Eleanor here too tonight?"

"Of course." Lolita barely looked at me. I knew she didn't like me and thought I was white trash. Well, what the fuck ever, I was, but at least we weren't in the trailer park anymore. And she was a fucking maid. How dare she judge me? I was fourteen, like I could really do much about my living situation at this time in my life.

"Thanks. We'll be upstairs for a while."

She gave him a hard look before nodding and walking away. I flipped her off when her back was to us, making me feel slightly better. Screw you, Lolita. That was a stripper name if I ever heard one. I bet she had a past.

"Come on." I followed Billy up the left side of the staircase, then down another hallway and into his bedroom, which was larger than the entire apartment Mom and I currently lived in. Three of our old trailers could fit in his room. Ah, to live the high life. I couldn't even imagine ever having the nice things he did.

He sat on his bed and I opened my backpack and took out the bong before sitting next to him. I pulled a baggie out of my backpack as well, producing the weed I swiped from Mom's stash before I left. We were quiet as he quickly and efficiently got our afternoon delight ready for us. Soon, we were in a cloud of marijuana haze and quickly started making out.

He tugged my shirt off me and I reached for his zipper, quickly getting him out of his jeans. He took another hit off the bong and blew the smoke back into my face before kissing me again, deeply. I let my drug-induced mind wander to delicious thoughts, like Billy falling in love with me and us living happily ever after. I would be saved. No Mom, none of her creepy fucking boyfriends who liked to fondle me when she was in the bathroom, shooting up. No more pain.

"Suck my dick, you whore," Billy whispered, grabbing me behind the head and forcing my face into his crotch. Or not. I was Billy's little secret, his slutty secret. I knew the arrangement. I provided the drugs and sex, he provided me food, cash, and little bit of shelter when I needed to get away. He didn't love me. He would never respect me. He just wanted my body.

I went to work, carefully moving my mouth up and down, fondling his balls just like I knew he liked. I flicked my eyes up to see him take another hit, then grab my face with both his hands and ease my head up and down. He liked being in control. And whatever. As long as I had some decent food today and he spotted me at least a hundred bucks, I would be happy. Billy was a senior and would be moving away to college in just five short months. What the fuck was I going to do without him? He was my best paying customer and really, our sex was great. He wasn't too big or too small, he wasn't into weird kinky shit like some other guys I fucked. He was my favorite. I loved his fucking house. I could come here and pretend I would one day be Mrs. Billy Bowlls, dripping in jewelry and hiring a housekeeper because I was just too busy and my house was too big to clean.

"Let me cum on your face," Billy grunted, before he pulled himself out of my mouth and aimed his dick right at my nose. Ah, yes, the worst part about Billy. He loved to relieve himself on my face, in my ear, on my ass crack. He couldn't just let me swallow like a normal fucking whore.

As I took his cum right in my face, I was reminded of who I really was. Eleanor Cauler. Daughter of a drug addict and whore. Like mother, like fucking daughter.

PRUE

15 Years Ago

In middle school, one of the popular girls asked me to sit at their lunch table one day. I can remember the butterflies I felt as I looked up from working on my English homework while eating the waffles and sweet potato fries and seeing Marley approach me, her shiny blonde hair swinging from side to side and her sparkling blue eyes focused right on me. I darted my eyes to the spaces next to me; no one was there. Why was she looking at me?

"Prue, right?" She slid in on the bench seat across from me, eyes focused only on me. I forced myself not to look behind me. I mean, she said my name.

"Yeah?" I asked, warily.

"Hi, I'm Marley." As if I didn't know. Everyone knew Marley.

"Hi." The hesitation was still in my voice.

"Do you want to come sit by us? You shouldn't have to eat alone."

It was November. I had been sitting alone at lunch nearly every day for three months.

"Oh. Well."

"Come on, let's go! I'll introduce you to the rest of the girls. They just love you!"

I highly doubted they even knew my name. I still couldn't figure out how Marley knew my name. Or why she suddenly cared.

The rest of her friends cheerily said hello to me as I sat down. They asked me questions—what book was I reading, how did I like my classes, was my family traveling over Christmas break? I felt . . . accepted. I felt like I made new friends that day. I wasn't super nerdy or unpopular, I just typically preferred to be by myself. I actually had a best friend, an old neighbor who moved to the other side of town at the beginning of eighth grade, and she now went to the other middle school. She was much more outgoing than me, and it was hard for me to break out of my shell without her for backup anymore.

Over the next two weeks, I felt like I had been best friends with Marley and crew forever. I started wearing makeup to school, had sleepovers at Marley's big fancy house, and always had a place at their lunch table. One week before we were to go on Christmas break, Marley asked me to go shopping with her at the local Micks, which was like a really small Target. She said her parents just gave her some allowance money to pick up a new swimming suit and other essentials she would need on her Bahamas cruise coming up.

After school on a Friday, we walked together, just the two of us, to Micks, which was about a ten-minute walk from school. She said her Mom would give me a ride home once we were finished, and we had one hour to find everything before her Mom showed up.

As we were walking, Marley reached into her backpack and pulled out two large purses. "I almost forgot. I got this for you." She handed me the black one.

I gingerly reached out for the purse. "What? Why?" I didn't use a purse, just my backpack or my pockets for anything I needed. The other girls carried purses outside of school, but I didn't see the point of them.

She rolled her eyes. "Come on, girl. You know why."

I stared blankly back at her. "Not really."

"Cause we are going shopping!" She flung her arms out enthusiastically as we approached the parking lot of Micks.

"I know that. But why are you giving me a purse?" I couldn't connect the dots.

Another eye roll. "Come on, Prue. We're going shopping—for free!"

She grabbed my hand and started dragging me to the front doors. Free shopping? What did that mean? Oh, wait. The pieces fell into place. "Wait. You want to *steal*?"

"It's not stealing. It's just a five-finger discount!"

The front doors opened and we walked inside, my stomach feeling weak. What? I couldn't steal. That was illegal. I would so be grounded—forever. Were you arrested for shoplifting?

"Marley," I hissed between my teeth as she headed for the clothing section. "I don't want to do this."

"Prue," she hissed back. "Grow up. Seriously. We do this all the time. It's no big deal."

She reached the juniors section and started looking through the swimsuits, grabbing several and then moving on to another rack. I stood by her, nervously shuffling my feet.

"I think I want to leave."

"And how are you going to get home? It's like a thirty-minute walk to your house. Come on, Prue. You don't always have to be such a goody goody." She narrowed her eyes at me.

My stomach clenched again. Why was she doing this?

What was the plan? Was this why she befriended me—to steal a few swimsuits? That was ridiculous.

She pulled me into the dressing room with her and undressed without abandon, put on two separate bikini tops and bottoms, then started to redress.

"What are you doing?" I asked loudly.

She turned quickly and glared at me, a finger over her lips. "Quiet! And help me get this tag off. I can't reach it."

Before I could help myself, I was ripping off the price tag on the second bikini top. After she was fully dressed, she grabbed the rest of the swimsuits and set them on the counter outside the dressing room area. I walked around in a daze as she stealthily slipped items into her open purse—shampoo, conditioner, hair dye, earrings.

"This is too heavy. Will you carry this?" She held out her purse full of contraband to me, and I shook my head.

"No way. I don't want to get caught."

The classic eye roll. "Look around. There are practically no employees here. That's why it's so easy. I need to take your purse. I'm not done yet."

I was numb as she grabbed the empty purse from me and swung the heavy purse onto my shoulder. I just wanted to get out. I knew this would end bad.

"Oh, hold on." She looked down at her watch, her forehead wrinkling in concern. "It's been an hour. My mom is probably outside."

She turned to head to the door, and I asked, "Isn't she going to think it's weird you've been here for an hour and didn't buy anything?"

She turned around, her blue eyes studying mine. "You're right." She grabbed a few items closest to her, which included Pringles and a pack of juice boxes, and headed to the cash register. "I'll pay for these. Will you go see if she's out there and tell her I'm coming?"

I started to leave the store when a hand came down on my shoulder. "Young lady. You're going to need to come with me."

I looked up to see a man with a pinched face looking at me, an employee name badge on his chest.

"Why?" I asked, suddenly scared.

He looked at the purse slung over my shoulder, and I suddenly realized I was still holding the purse full of stolen items. Marley had the empty purse as she was checking out with her snacks.

"No. This isn't mine. It belongs to my friend," I said, my voice weak.

"Young lady. Let's go."

I saw a flash of Marley as I was led into the security office. She was smirking at me, then calmly turned and left the store with her empty purse, bag of snacks—and stolen swimwear under her clothes. That must have been all she really came for. The manager pulled in a security guard and called the police, who came and estimated the value of stolen goods at over $300. My parents were called and I tried to explain to them what happened, and while I think maybe they believed me, I was still grounded for a month, which meant no social time over Christmas break. They called Marley's parents to get her side of the story, and her mom told my mom that Marley never even went to Micks that day, that she didn't pick her up, and that her child had done nothing wrong.

I guess Marley tried to get away with stealing and

used me as a fallback in case she was caught—or rather, I was caught. She never talked to me again once we were back in school, and her clique didn't even bother to pretend like they knew my name anymore. I saw her befriend and unfriend others like me and wondered how she used them. I couldn't worry about the others, though. I was just lucky I was under eighteen and wouldn't have a permanent record, like the police officer at Micks so kindly informed me as she lectured me on shoplifting.

Chapter 3

NELLIE

Present Day

Our housekeeper, Maria, was still at the house when I got home from the tanning salon. Harrison's car wasn't in the garage, so I assumed he was either working late or off at the gym. Why he bothered with a gym membership when we had our own private gym at the house was beyond me. The one time I questioned it, he said it was about supporting local businesses. My bad.

"Good evening, Mrs. Hawthorne. You have good day?" Maria asked me as I entered the kitchen.

"Oh, hi, Maria. Yes, yes, busy day." I paused, and then remembered I needed to ask her a question. Sometimes I still needed to remind myself how to be a good human being. I looked up again, a smile on my lips this time. "Big plans for the weekend?"

Her eyes lit up and she started talking about her

family from Chicago who was coming out to visit her. Her English wasn't great and when she was excited she talked fast, so it was hard to follow along. But I tried.

Fifteen minutes later, she was finally heading out the door, waving cheerfully to me as she walked to the end of our block and took a right, heading toward the bus stop. We paid her enough that she could afford a car, but she insisted she didn't want one, even after Harrison offered to help her go to the dealership and make sure she got a good deal and wasn't taken advantage of. That was my husband. Always Mr. Nice Guy. And he made me a nicer person. Just another reason I loved him.

I went upstairs to shower and change. By the time I got out and was standing wrapped in a fluffy towel, staring into my walk-in closet, my phone chimed. Harrison. Freaking finally.

At gym. Be home in 20. Order some food please?

So we weren't going out. I selected a pair of pink yoga pants, purple sports bra, and pink racerback tank. I would hit up our home gym after eating dinner. Another Friday night in my exciting life. Dinner with my husband, then working out, then going to bed. Probably without having sex either. When Harrison was gone all day and night, he was exhausted by the time we got to bed. What fun.

Just before eight, Harrison finally made it home. The Chinese food I ordered had been delivered twenty minutes earlier, as Harrison was twenty minutes late.

"It should still be warm," I said as he walked into the kitchen, taking a bite of sweet and sour chicken. I made the executive decision not to wait for him after he was ten minutes late.

"Sorry. I got held up by a group of guys just as I was leaving. I didn't want to seem rude," he said, coming over and dropping a kiss on the top of my head before grabbing his box of chicken and broccoli.

I tried to smile. Always considerate Harrison Hawthorne. "That's okay, babe. How was your day?"

We had the usual dinner conversation, talking about our day, our work, the people we talked to. I ate at a steady pace, knowing moderation was key, especially if I was working out right after. Nothing like overstuffing myself and then barely being able to move and wasting my Friday night staring morosely at the television set and repainting my toenails.

"Big plans for the night?" Harrison asked, walking to the fridge to refill his jug of water. His new health kick these days meant the water jug went with him everywhere, as he tried to get as much water down throughout the day. It was actually a rule that I went by too, but I used the more appropriate tumblers than the oversized pail he lugged around.

I shrugged. "Just going to get in a workout, that's about all. Yourself?"

"I need to look over a few reports, but that's all. Before I forget, Mom invited us over for dinner next Thursday night. Will that work for you?"

I mentally reviewed my schedule. "That should be fine." Oh joy, dinner with my mother-in-law. Vernie Hawthorne was about the most overprotective, over-the-top mother I had ever been around. Maybe we just didn't get along because I wasn't used to her parenting style at all. Not even after two years of marriage.

"Good. I'll call her tonight to confirm." Harrison's family lived just four blocks away from us, but we had to book a week out to have dinner with them. The formality would never make sense to me.

After dinner, I went to our gym while Harrison retreated to his office. I gave it my all for ninety minutes—cardio, Pilates, cardio, Yoga. As I did my last sun salutation and then my last child's pose, I actually felt at peace. I was new to the yoga practice, and maybe there was more to this yoga thing than I gave it credit for. Yes, it helped keep me trim and toned and flexible in bed, but I actually felt . . . better when I completed a workout. My mind slowed down. I felt calmer, more steady.

I cleaned off my equipment, rolled up my yoga mat, and turned the lights off, grabbing my water bottle and towel and heading upstairs. Just as I walked through the main level, our front door opened and Harrison walked in, sweaty and wearing running shoes.

"Did you go for a run?" I asked, surprised. Why would he run when he already went to the gym?

"Yeah, just a quick one around the block. I only lifted at the gym and still wanted to get a run in."

He peeled off his sweaty shirt and I got a good look at his defined stomach. Since he started his workout/healthy lifestyle kick, his body had definitely changed. I'd never known Harrison to be remotely overweight, but he started to get a little soft after our wedding. A beer belly had started to appear. I felt a little guilty for the change, since one night about a year ago I poked him in the stomach and made the Pillsbury Doughboy noise. I was totally kidding and thought he would get my joke, but he actually just got offended. Slowly, over time, he made little changes. Cutting back on soda and beer, slashing out fast food, including his favorite Big Macs, and working out more. The past few months it had been amped up even more.

"Oh, okay. I'm going to go shower." I walked toward the stairs when I felt his hand on my waist. I turned, right before he swooped down and kissed me passionately. Well, this was different. I let myself fall into his embrace, swinging my arms around his neck and pressing my body against his. Our sweaty bodies slid together, him with no shirt, me in only a sports bra.

"Let's get into that shower," he murmured, burying his face in my neck.

"Together?" I asked, in somewhat disbelief. We didn't shower together anymore. It just seemed a little pointless and silly. So different from our early days of dating.

"Yes," he whispered, before picking me up and racing up the stairs with me in his arms.

I laughed, not sure what was coming over my husband. This was so unlike him. But I loved it. We had grown too comfortable and it was starting to make me bored. I didn't know how to bring it up, though, because it wasn't necessarily a bad thing. But he was slowly morphing into his dad. And that was a little weird. And as Harrison started putting more and more pressure on me for children, I felt like all my carefully hidden secrets would start spilling at some point. I didn't—couldn't—be humiliated in this town, in front of our friends and acquaintances. And now the new man in town.

Those thoughts all but disappeared as we made love in the shower, then again in the bedroom. I went to bed that night snuggled against my husband, feeling so conflicted. I loved him, loved the life we had started to build together. But that text message hiding on my phone wouldn't let me forget that everything could soon implode.

* * *

Another Monday morning. I woke up at five, brushing my teeth and securing my hair back in a ponytail. I went downstairs to the gym and popped in Jillian Michaels Yoga Meltdown DVD. I was getting the double whammy with this—yoga plus an ass whooping by Jillian. Thirty minutes later, I hopped on the treadmill and put the mode on hill climb, the resistance increasing every five minutes as I walked at a brisk pace. My legs were burning once I got off thirty minutes later, and I scooped up my water bottle and towel, heading upstairs to shower.

Harrison was just waking as I stepped out, getting dressed for the day in a lavender dress cut at the knees with a wide leather belt and long earrings. I felt like being pretty and feminine today, as our last summer days started to wind down. Pretty soon it would be all about leather jackets and leggings and boots, but for now, I relished the summer dresses.

"You look nice," Harrison complimented, sitting up in bed.

I beamed at my husband. We had a truly terrific weekend together. It felt like something had shifted these past few days. Instead of acting like we were roommates, we acted like a happily married couple. We went to lunch in downtown Chicago on Saturday and then caught a night game at Wrigley Field, totally spur of the moment.

Harrison bought tickets from an older gentleman standing outside the famous stadium, and we noshed on pretzels and hot dogs and twelve-dollar beers. We made love again that night, and on Sunday morning before we made pancakes together and enjoyed them on the deck in the back.

It was such a nice, unexpected weekend. I wasn't sure what was accounting for the change—was it Harrison? Me? I honestly didn't think I was doing anything different, but . . . maybe I was. Maybe I was just proving to myself that I could do this. I could be the wife of Harrison Hawthorne and keep it together. I was always going to feel guilty that I duped my husband. That he didn't know the real me, my actual past. That my lies could affect our future together. But . . . I could get around that. Maybe. Possibly. But I could try. This weekend proved that we were good together. Our marriage wasn't going stale. I wouldn't get bored and run. That was always my biggest fear when I agreed to get married.

Guess who's coming to town! Okay, it's me. I've missed you babe. I'm moving to Oamark Park in two weeks. Up for a friendly reunion?

I looked at the text on my phone, from Calvin. From my past. Shit. Why was he moving here? And why did he want to see me again? I broke off our . . . thing right before I got married. I wanted to start my marriage right. I wanted to mean my vows. Harrison was my everything. Sure, I freaked out a little before the wedding. But that was me. A fucked-up girl with a fucked-up past. I was willing to settle down, to be the tame Mrs. that Harrison thought I wanted to be. Can you blame me for going a little insane before the wedding band went on my finger?

Two weeks before I said "I do," I broke it off with Calvin, told him to forget me, and then immediately after our big Chicago wedding, we moved to Oamark Park and I left Calvin and his memories behind. How did he know I moved here? Had he looked me up? And what was he planning to do about it? I could just imagine what could happen if Calvin showed up at the house one night with a boombox on one shoulder and professing his love to me. I shuddered.

I parked my car in the lot and opened the door. Kerri was behind the desk as usual, smiling brightly at me.

"Hi, Nellie! I know it's early in the season but they just came out and I had to get you one, too!" She pulled out a Starbucks cup from under the desk and handed it to me. "Your first pumpkin spice latte of the year!"

I had to laugh. "Thanks, Kerri. Do you think this is the year that you convert me?"

"I'm going to give it my all." We laughed together.

Kerri was a huge fan of Starbucks, or Starbies as she affectionately called the coffeehouse giant. I just couldn't get into it, but each season she tried to hook me on a new drink. This summer it was the Refreshers, which I admit, were pretty good. I had bought a few myself without the urging of Kerri, and she was thrilled each time I told her what I had done.

But a pumpkin spice latte tasted like I was drinking a pot of cinnamon . . . with a little bit of pumpkin flavoring. Just not for me. I would discreetly dump it when Kerri wasn't around.

I took a small sip to appease one of my best workers

and then raised my cup in a cheers motion. "I'll be in my office if you need me."

She acknowledged me with a head tilt and then sat behind the desk, clicking away on the computer.

I walked into my office, setting the PSL on the desk and then my cell phone. I picked it up, found Calvin's text, then logged onto our cell phone provider's website. I blocked his number from our phones, then sat back in my chair with a sigh.

NELLIE

20 Years Ago

I first noticed the differences in my mom when I was about nine years old. She seemed somewhat normal up until then —she flitted from job to job, but she always remembered to pick me up from school, she had a car, and even sometimes she came into my classrooms as a volunteer. But then, something changed. It wasn't like a switch was flipped. No, it was more gradual. And I had no idea what had triggered it, or how to get us back to normal.

I was in fourth grade, waiting outside school for the third time that week for Mom to get me. Mrs. Limal, my teacher, came up beside me, touching my shoulder.

"She must have forgot. Again," I mumbled, feeling embarrassed. No one else was left behind after school.

"Why don't you ride with me, then? I'm happy to drop you off. Do you think your mom is at home?"

I started to shake my head no, then stopped. If I said no, would she leave me here? "Probably. Sometimes she sleeps a lot." At least that was the truth.

"Okay, then. Why don't you follow me?"

I followed silently behind my teacher, wanting to kick myself for standing outside school like a dummy. Mom was late the first day this week, pretty late the second, really late the third, but now . . . I guessed it was even later than late if the teachers were leaving. I tested out a new word on my tongue that I heard Mom and her new friends say all the time. *Fuck.* I said it once on the playground and got in trouble because a teacher overheard me. So I knew it was bad. I liked bad words. So did my mom, and her friends.

I climbed into the little car, folding my legs in and shutting the door behind me. Mrs. Limal tried to keep chattering on the drive, but I didn't respond much. I just didn't know what to say. And didn't care. I just wanted to be home.

When she pulled up to my house, I reached for the door handle.

"I can walk you to your door," she said, reaching for her purse in the backseat.

"It's okay," I said quickly. I had no idea if she was home or not, but what if she wasn't? Where would Mrs. Limal take me?

She frowned. "I should really make sure she's here before I leave you alone."

"I can take care of myself. I do sometimes." Clearly, those were the wrong words to say, because her frown just deepened. *Fuck.* "I mean, just when she goes to the gas station right there." I pointed to the gas station visible from our house.

"Well . . ."

I could tell she was about to argue more, when our front door opened. Mom came down the walk, waving like it was a normal thing, having her daughter dropped off by a teacher because she forgot.

"Oh, good." Mrs. Limal looked relieved.

"I am so sorry," Mom said once she reached the car. I pushed the door open and got out, holding my book bag awkwardly. "I worked the graveyard shift and forgot to set my alarm. Thank you so much for bringing her home." She hugged me to her, and I tried not to wince at the smell coming off her. Gross.

"That's quite all right, Mrs. Cauler. Happy to help out today." She paused, looking over me and my mom, standing there on our porch in front of the rundown shack we called home. "Are you all right? Can I help with anything?"

"I'm just fine, thank you for asking. We'll just head in and heat up the casserole I made yesterday for dinner tonight."

I twisted my head to look at her. What casserole? She didn't make anything last night. She didn't even come home last night, and I put myself to bed after doing my homework. Maybe she made it when I was sleeping?

Mrs. Limal seemed hesitant to leave. "All right, then," she finally said, turning to leave. "Nellie, I'll see you in school tomorrow."

"Bye, Mrs. Limal. Thank you for the ride," I said in a soft voice, for some reason not wanting my teacher to leave.

She gave my mom a long look before turning completely and walking back to her car. Mom turned me around and we walked inside the house, Mom immediately sitting on the couch and picking up a cigarette that was burning in a cigarette tray. Napping, huh? I didn't think Mom was that dumb to sleep with a lit cigarette in the house.

"Um, Mom? That casserole?" I asked timidly. My stomach was growling after having to wait so long at school.

"Make yourself a sandwich if you're hungry. I have a friend coming over any minute."

The doorbell rang as she said those words.

"Shoo. Go get some food and do your homework in your room. I'm busy."

I obediently went into the kitchen, grabbed a bag of Cheetos puffs and a bottle of half-drunk water from the fridge. I didn't know what she meant by sandwich. We hadn't had any bread in weeks. And Doritos and cheese sandwiches were my favorite.

I was heading down the little hallway to my room when I heard a man's voice. Another of Mom's "friends." I wished my bedroom door had a lock on it.

Later that evening, I was reading a book, trying to get lost into a world filled with the coolest baby-sitters around, when my door creaked open. My heart froze, but I relaxed when I saw Mom peeking her head through.

"Goodnight, schewheawrt," she slurred, her eyes barely open.

"Night, Mom," I said, not bothering to look up again from the printed words.

I noticed out of the corner of my eye that she started to fall backwards and almost raised my head until I saw her "friend" catch her. Without a word, he dragged her away, and I heard her bedroom door creak open, then minutes later his grunts and some pounding against the wall.

I shuddered, reaching underneath my bed for the cotton balls that I snagged out of the school nurse's office last week for instances like these. I hated the noises.

Later that night, I was awoken by someone towering over me. A book was on my chest and I still had the cotton balls in my ears. I sleepily opened my eyes, seeing Mom's "friend" standing over me, a vicious look in his eyes.

I knew what was coming before my brain could even fully awaken. I kept the cotton balls in so I could muffle his noises, the same ones he had made with my mother just hours before.

PRUE

9 Years Ago

The beginning of my college years, I was really good friends with three girls—Amanda, Carli, and Joelle. We bonded nearly instantly at freshman orientation, and by the time second semester rolled around, I considered them my best friends.

Carli backed out of our New Year's Eve plan during our sophomore year, which was to go to a house party thrown by a bunch of guys. Always up for a party, Amanda, Joelle, and myself speculated why she wouldn't be going. Carli claimed she needed to practice (she was also in school for court reporting, which was a very tough major) but her whole attitude seemed off.

One day while in Carli's room, I noticed a flyer half sticking out of her dresser when I went through her bedroom to use the bathroom. Since it was on my way, I grabbed the flyer to set it back on top, when I noticed what it was—and it explained Carli's suddenly bailing on parties and her demeanor change.

I kept the news of finding out Carli was pregnant to myself. I figured she was still making the decision of what to do, and she would tell us at her own time. She had only just recently begun dating Xavier, so there was also that to consider. And there was no way she could finish a court reporter degree while pregnant. The hours we had to put in were insane and time off was practically unheard of.

I worried about Carli for the next two weeks but kept a smile on my face when I was around her and the other girls. I kept my struggle internal, even though it was now clearly obvious to me Carli was pregnant. Her boobs were huge, her perky attitude was dulled, and she was eating some weird stuff and drinking healthy smoothies, which she never touched previously.

Amanda and Joelle pulled me aside on a Friday morning as I was leaving a classroom. They were giggling together and made a big show of looking around and making sure no one was paying attention to us.

"What's up?" I asked, confused by their behavior.

"We have some news. Or possible news. We have a suspicion," Amanda said, her dark eyes alight.

"Okkkkay."

"We think Carli is pregnant!" Joelle squealed, then quickly darted her eyes around again to make sure no one overheard her loud whisper.

I looked at my friends, wondering why they were so giddy over the news. Had they not thought it out? That Carli might have to drop out of school? That she might be scared, upset? Why were they acting so . . . dramatic?

"Okkkkay," I repeated, as we kept walking.

"I don't know why she's trying to hide it from us; we're her best friends. So we're going to *make* her tell us," Amanda said.

"How?"

"We're having a girls' night tonight, and we'll just keep bugging her to drink and take shots and stuff. She'll eventually cave."

I wasn't happy with this plan. "Guys, what if she's not happy about it? What if she's not saying anything because she isn't ready yet, or doesn't have a plan? I think we should give her more time."

"So you think she's pregnant, too? How come you didn't say anything?" Joelle pouted.

"Because there's nothing to say. Give her some space. Pregnancy is a huge deal. It's not something to force someone to tell."

They just rolled their eyes at me, and sure enough, that night poor Carli tried to dodge the drinks and shot requests, sipping slowly on a bottle of beer and disappearing into the bathroom with her drinks all night. I felt sick to my own stomach imagining what she must be going through, but I didn't know what to do. I was caught in the middle of friends, and I knew this would turn out badly.

Sure enough, at the end of the night during the silent cab ride back home, I could see Carli was crying silently, her hands tightly clenched together. I promised myself I would talk to her once we got back to campus, to try to help her.

Once we were back on campus, Amanda and Joelle decided to hit up another apartment where a bunch of our guy friends (and their occasional hookups) were hanging out. I asked Carli if I could walk her back to her room, and we were silent all the way there.

Once inside, she suddenly flung her purse to the ground and shouted at me. "What the hell was that, Prue?"

I was completely taken aback. "What? What are you talking about?"

"Why were you practically force-feeding me alcohol tonight? What's your problem?"

"Me?" I gestured to myself pathetically, wishing the

other two were with me now. Why was she solely blaming me?

"Yes, you. What's the deal, huh? Just tell me!"

"Carli, I think you need to calm down. I think there's been a misunderstanding."

Her chest was heaving, and all I saw in her eyes was anger. "Just tell me what the fuck, Prue."

I tried to explain. I felt ridiculous, pinning the blame on Amanda and Joelle when they weren't there, like I was just using them as an escape plan. But I wasn't. It was the truth. But Carli had her mind made up.

"I thought you were a real friend, Prue. I never expected that kind of behavior from you. Thanks for throwing it in my face tonight that everything is going to change. Yeah, I'm dropping out of school. Yeah, Xavier and I are going to try to make this work, but who knows how that will end up? We'll probably be unhappy if we stay together, but now that we have a child to raise, we'll always be in each other's lives even though we've only been together for three months and slept with each other five times. My parents are furious, my future is totally fucked, and I can't even get the support of my best friend to be there for me. Thanks for making a mockery of my situation, Prue. See yourself out."

And with that, she stalked into the bedroom and slammed the door. I shakily let myself out and back to my own apartment, where I cried myself to sleep. It physically hurt that one of my best friends was so mad at me, and that it wasn't my fault. I tried to talk Amanda and Joelle out of it. Why was I the one being punished?

Amanda and Joelle denied knowing Carli was

pregnant, and for who knows what reason, she bought it. Even though it was those two trying to get her to drink all night and me being the silent fourth wheel, the three of them completely ditched me after that whole debacle. I lost three best friends in one night, all because of a misunderstanding and an unplanned pregnancy. How was that fair?

Chapter 4

PRUE

Present Day

I snapped Clemmie's leash on her and grabbed my sunglasses. We made for the door, Clemmie's tail going a mile a minute. This girl and walks.

We started on our usual route—out the parking lot of the apartment complex, heading west. The September air was crisp but not quite cold. Just enough to let us know that fall was here and summer would soon turn into a distant memory.

Clemmie continued to wiggle as we walked, her entire body showing her approval. One day, hopefully in the nearer future, I would get a house. She missed her big yard so much, and a dog of Clemmie's size shouldn't be stuck indoors all day.

My mind flashed back to Friday, when I was in the office. Deacon and Brandi were both there, making the office atmosphere nearly unbearable. It was like the other co-workers didn't know how to act with all three of us breathing the same air, and it was just plain uncomfortable. We had a mandatory meeting, though, and I couldn't get out of it, so I had no other choice but to take the train in on Friday morning and suffer until the meeting wrapped. I declined the invitation to go out to lunch with everyone after.

Linds, a fellow court reporter that I considered a close friend, met me in the bathroom before I could head out.

"Are you sure you can't come out with us?" she'd asked, running her hands under the faucet.

"Sorry, but no. That meeting was bad enough."

She'd nodded. "I understand. Do you want to get together sometime, though? I miss you."

I felt mad at that moment. Why did I have to feel uncomfortable at my job? Why did I have to not see my friends anymore? Why me? What had I ever done to deserve this?

I had to blink hard to keep the tears at bay. "Sure, Linds. I miss you, too."

"How about tomorrow? Come back into town. The Cubs and Cardinals start a series, and it's bound to be crazy. It'll be fun."

I had agreed. Baseball was huge around these parts, obviously. With the Chicago Cubs and White Sox rivalry, plus the Cubs looking like they might head to the playoffs this year by some miracle, everyone was hopped up on all things baseball. I liked the sport, but I wasn't insane about it like some people, Linds included. But I still agreed, because it would be something fun to do.

Clemmie sniffed out a pink flower that seemed to have randomly sprouted on a curb, then promptly ate it.

"Clemmie! You silly girl. We don't eat flowers." I bent down, trying to get the flower out of her mouth, but she swallowed before I could grab it and grinned at me—I swear. "Silly girl," I murmured again, then straightened and gasped.

"I'm so sorry! I didn't mean to scare you." It was Running Guy.

"That's okay," I gasped out. "Just startled a bit is all."

I desperately wanted to smooth down my hair, but I didn't want to make it obvious that I was thinking vain thoughts.

"Did she get something?" he asked, looking at me kindly.

"Oh, just a flower. Nothing too crazy," I managed to get out.

He squatted down so he was at Clem's level. "You're such a pretty dog," he said, scratching her behind the ears. She responded by resting her big head on his shoulder, which made him laugh.

"She's a lover, that's for sure," I said, smiling at the image.

"She's very pretty. Even when she is eating flowers," he responded, standing back up. "I'm Harrison."

I shook his proffered hand. "Prue. And this is Clementine, but I usually call her Clemmie or Clem."

"That's a nice name."

I just smiled, not sure if he meant mine or Clem's. I'm assuming it was the canine's because what was so special about Prue? I was just glad I could shorten my name, because Prudence? That was my great-grandmother's name, and while I did think it was pretty, it was just old-fashioned enough to make me not want to say it.

"Well, I'd better keep moving along. Got goals to hit," Harrison said, glancing at his Fitbit on his wrist.

"Are you training or something?" I asked.

"Not for anything in particular at this moment. Just trying to get into better shape, so I created a workout plan for myself and I like to stick to it." He looked down at his running shoes. "Probably silly, but it helps keep me motivated and on track."

"That's not silly at all. That's smart."

"Thanks."

We paused, and the silence was broken by Clem deciding it was time for us to move on, and she started pulling on the leash.

"Well, good luck with running," I said awkwardly, not sure how to end this encounter.

"Thanks. Have a good walk. Try to lay off the flowers, Clementine."

We laughed, and with little waves, we kept on our respective routes. I made sure not to look back, just in case he was possibly looking back and would catch me. Even though that meant I would technically be catching him. But what if I was looking first and then he looked, effectively catching me? Geez, listen to me! What was I, a high schooler?

I pushed Clem to go four miles, mostly lost in my daydreams during that time. Harrison. So Running Guy finally had a name. I had run into him three other times.

The first time was just a simple hello, the second time we saw each other we commented on the weather in passing, and the third time he had petted Clemmie and said she was a good-looking dog. But this was the first time we had really stopped to talk to one another, and we had even exchanged names. That was a pretty big deal, right? Did love stories really start that way? I'd heard of people finding love in like dog parks, but just on a walk?

I shook my head as I opened the door to the complex. Love? I literally just found out this guy's name—first name only—and I was already thinking love. How pathetic was that?

"You need to get a good rebound fling going," Linds had informed me on Sunday, when we were in Wrigleyville, drinking margaritas and watching the Cubs/Cards on one of the many TVs in the bar.

I had wrinkled my nose. "I don't know, Linds. That's not really my style."

"Rebound flings always help. And you need that buffer. You can't just go from one serious relationship to the next. You need that fun guy in the middle. It's just the right thing to do."

Maybe Running Guy—Harrison—could be my rebound guy? But . . . he didn't feel like a rebound guy to me.

I unclipped Clem from her leash and took off my tennis shoes. Maybe I could have a real conversation with this dude first before I started thinking too far into the future.

* * *

Thursday at one o'clock, I entered the tanning salon for my usual appointment. I checked in, grabbed a towel, and went to room 13. After removing all my clothes and slathering myself with the lotion, I grabbed my eyewear and lay on the bed, feeling like a vampire in a coffin as I closed myself in.

Tanning was my bad habit. I didn't drink frequently, I didn't smoke, I was practically a vegetarian though not 100% because I liked chicken. But tanning had been my vice after everything fell apart with Deacon. It was ten minutes to just be alone. I could take a catnap, I could devise my work schedule, I could create a mental grocery list. Tanning was my crutch right now. Hopefully when I was finally over my life completely falling apart, I could give it up. I knew tanning wasn't good for the body. But neither were a lot of other things, and I didn't do those.

And maybe one day I wouldn't feel like I had to justify myself every time I went tanning.

Lying in the bed, feeling the warmth spreading throughout my body, I got lost in thoughts of my past life. How did I not see Deacon for who he really was? How was I fooled that badly?

Three years. Three years I put myself all in for that relationship. Deacon was my best friend. How was I to know he would break my heart? How did I know someone who passed herself off as my friend would sleep with my boyfriend? How could either of them look themselves in the mirror after what they did?

And when would karma stick it to them?

No, that wasn't the right way to think. I listened to the hum of the bed and was surprised when I felt the wetness on my face. Why did the sessions always include crying? I didn't even realize I was shedding tears until I felt them dripping down my face.

But it's just so unfair. One day, I wanted to figure out what the heck I did to deserve Deacon and Brandi to dupe me like that. To break my heart, and my trust, like that.

I dressed quickly after my ten minutes were up, wiping the tears from my face still. As I gathered up my belongings and left the room, I heard a woman call out to me as I was nearing the front door.

"Thanks for coming in, Prue."

I turned at the sound of my name and lifted a hand to the familiar-looking woman standing behind the desk. She looked at me with concern, and I realized she could tell I was crying.

I hurried out, embarrassed, and ran to my car.

Chapter 5

NELLIE

I watched Prue hurry out the door, then break into a run before she got to her car. I shook my head as I headed back to her room to clean up. What was that woman's story? It was just so weird.

My phone lit up and I stopped thinking of the strange customer when I saw Harrison's name on the screen.

Dinner tonight?

Yeah. What are you thinking? I thumbed back.

Anne and Gus asked if we wanted to come over.

My nose wrinkled. Oh goodie. A suburb dinner with boring accountant Gus and his even duller wife. Sounds like a hoot.

Fine by me! I included the exclamation mark to try to prove to myself, too, that I was happy about this arrangement. It would be a bland dinner with even blander conversations, and I'm sorry, but their kids freaked me out. They were like Stepford kids or something. It was weird.

But, it would all be okay. We would make it through dinner, and then be rewarded with dessert once we were home.

* * *

"Come on, Harrison. Even you have to admit those kids are kooky."

I walked through our front door and slipped my heels off, my feet aching, my big toes pinched. No one says Louboutin heels are comfortable. No really. No one says that.

"They're just polite. They have good manners. That doesn't make them kooky," Harrison protested, removing his suit jacket.

"They literally do not talk unless spoken to. What kids do you know do that? Huh?" I challenged him, but with a smile on my face.

The dinner went just as I thought—mind-numbingly boring, and a little on the scary side because of those kids. Were they even real?

"I can assure you our children won't be that way," Harrison said, coming over and putting his hands on my hips. "With you as their mother, they'll have a little saucy side in them."

I reached up on my tiptoes to place a kiss on his lips, even though my heart was starting to beat faster.

"Shall we take this to bedroom?" I tried to ask seductively.

"Practicing all ready?" he murmured, moving his

mouth to my ear.

I hoped he didn't catch my nervous laughter. "Let's just see where the night takes us."

After, when we were lying in each other's arms, I could hear Harrison's light snores and finally relaxed a little. Harrison had stopped the persistent children talk months ago, when he started getting into his whole fitness craze, but apparently, he was back on that horse now. Fucking great.

I wiggled out of his arms and rolled over on my side, too tired to get up and put clothes on. Sleeping naked didn't bother me, even though I knew I would feel cold in the morning and wake up to another sex session. Not that I minded the sex, but I had to get Harrison's attentions off children again. But how?

I drifted to sleep, my thoughts tumbling around and around.

* * *

Friday morning, Harrison made us both breakfast before we had to head our respective ways. I woke up early like usual and went to the basement for my workout—a mixture of Yoga and Pilates today, with a quick fifteen minutes on a 40% incline with the trusty treadmill—and Harrison went out jogging.

"Doesn't the cold bother you when you run?" I asked when we were both in the kitchen, showered and dressed for work.

"Nah." He flipped an egg in the pan with ease. "I just need to wear a hat now or my ears hurt at the end. But I like the cold over being too warm and sticky at the end."

Within minutes I was digging into breakfast. "Thanks for cooking this morning," I said, taking a small bite of eggs. I skipped the toast but buttered a piece for Harrison.

"My pleasure, dear wife."

I smiled. Everything was going so well. If only Calvin would finally just give up and move on to someone who could actually be in a relationship with him. And if . . .

"So, do you think we should have this discussion now?" Harrison asked, sitting down across from me with his own plate.

"What discussion?" Even though my stomach flipped, I knew what was coming next.

"The baby talk."

My smile tightened. "What do you want to talk about?"

"Come on, Nellie. We've been married almost three years. We're obviously financially stable. I think it's something we should start to seriously consider."

I took a deep breath. "Okay. I'll consider it."

Harrison watched me closely. "What does that mean?"

"What?"

"What does that mean? You'll consider it . . . today? This week?"

"Now I have to map out a timeline for you?" I snapped.

"Nell, what's going on? Have you changed your mind about having children?"

"No. I just." I blew out a breath. "I don't know. I just can't picture it yet. It's so . . . life changing. So final."

"Final?"

"All the changes we would have to make. It's not just like switching to a new car or even buying a house. It's forever."

"But it would be our forever." My husband reached over and grabbed my hand. "Just picture it—our own little family, finally being started. Our own son or daughter to raise the way we want to. Our own mini-mes running around the house. A new adventure for us."

My heart felt like it was being squeezed. I knew Harrison wanted children, but I didn't think he wanted them this bad. He had dropped hints shortly after our wedding, but we were so busy putting our new house together and getting the tanning salon open that it was always on the back burner. But now . . . I knew he was serious about this. So what the fuck did that mean for me? For us?

I tried to smile and squeezed his hand back. "I'll think very seriously about it. I . . . I promise. It's just a big change. That's all."

We finished eating our breakfast quietly, then kissed each other good-bye before we both left. I only made it a block before I pulled over in a CVS parking lot, my hands shaking badly. Fuck. Fuck. My lies were catching up with me. My past was catching up with me.

I took a few deep breaths to get myself under control, then decided to run into the CVS for a soda to calm my stomach and maybe some chocolate—which I only allowed in my weak moments. Now was one of them.

Inside, I was just making my way to the cash register when I heard a familiar voice call my name. My blood froze.

"Nellie. I thought that was you. How are you?"

It was Calvin. I turned slowly on my heel, my thoughts racing.

"Calvin. Hello. Long time no see." That was the best I could come up with.

"Yeah. So . . . I take it from the silence you got married?"

I held up my left hand, showing off my wedding ring. "I did."

"Wow. Good for you." His tone said otherwise.

I nodded curtly. "Look, Calvin, I'm happily married now." I cut my eyes around the store, making sure no one, especially a nosy neighbor of mine, was around to witness me talking to him. "And I would appreciate it if the past stayed in the past. Where it belongs."

His lips curled up into a small smile. "Of course, Nellie. What do you think I'm going to do?"

I didn't know. That was the worst part. Calvin had been locked away for over two years. His sudden appearance made me uneasy, thrown off my game. Everything was perfect now, the way it was supposed to be. The way I worked so hard for it to be. I couldn't have one man mess up my life.

"I'm glad you agree. I need to get to work."

"Nellie!" His voice called out after me, and I slowly turned again. He waved a hand. "Don't be shy, stranger."

Fuck me.

Chapter 6

PRUE

"Prue, dear?"

I rolled over in bed, phone to my ear. "Yes, Mother. I can come in today."

"Thank you so much, darling. We'll need lunch and library today if your schedule allows it."

"Not a problem. I'll see you in a few hours." I hung up and groaned. I just wanted to sleep. Linds somehow convinced me to go out again last night, for the Bears Sunday Night Football game. Now I was regretting that fourth cocktail on a light dinner.

Clemmie licked my face, making me smile. "Oh, girl. Are you ready for the week? Are you ready, my big bear? Are you?" She licked my face eagerly, telling me either she was ready for the week or she just had to pee.

"Okay, my girl. I'm up! Let me brush my teeth." I

shuffled in the bathroom to find my toothbrush because my teeth felt like a sweater was keeping them warm. My head was pounding, and while I was furiously brushing, I opened the medicine cabinet to find some ibuprofen. This is why I didn't drink much. Feeling like crud in the morning and the hangover effects were not my idea of fun.

After brushing my teeth, I swished some water quickly in my mouth and swallowed the pills. Throwing on a pair of slippers, I hooked Clem to her leash and walked her outside, letting her do her business before coming back in and putting food in her dish, then making myself a Pop-Tart. While I waited for it to warm in the toaster, I took an apple out of the fridge and sliced it. A balanced breakfast.

Glancing at the clock, I saw I had under three hours to walk Clem, shower, and feel like a normal person. Ugh. I quickly ate half the apple, until my stomach started to roll. I threw the few extra slices in the trash. No use trying to save an apple once sliced. It was already turning brown.

I slipped my shoes on and wrapped the strawberry Pop-Tart in a napkin, and Clem and I were out the door, heading west.

We walked for about fifteen minutes when I saw a man jogging toward us. Could it be?

Harrison quickly came into view, and my heartbeat sped up. Would he stop and say hi again?

Clemmie was clearly on my side, because she decided to stop then and pee. During that break, Harrison jogged right up to us.

"Prue and Clementine! How are you ladies this lovely Monday morning?" He sounded so much peppier than I felt—and probably looked.

I let out a little laugh. "One of us had a late night last night, so we're in rough shape this morning."

"Oh no. Clementine, did you hit the bottle a little too hard last night? Eat too many rawhides?"

I laughed. "Yep, it was totally her. She's a rule breaker."

"I would ask if you were having fun, but usually a hangover means it was a good night," Harrison said, smiling. I couldn't get over how blue his eyes were. They were just . . . pretty. But in a manly way.

"Just watching the Bears get stomped with a girlfriend. But yeah, it was a decent night."

He grimaced. "That game was ugly. At least our Cubbies have something brewing this year."

"Are you a big baseball fan?" I asked, trying to keep cool. This was more than just a passing friendly chat. This was a real conversation.

"I wouldn't say I'm the biggest fan out there, but I follow it. And cheer on the Cubs each year, though this is one of the first years in a while that I don't feel embarrassed saying that."

We smiled at each other, understanding that pain of being a Cubs fan. It had been a rough . . . century.

"Well—"

"Are you—"

We laughed as we spoke over one another.

"Go ahead," Harrison said.

"I was just going to say I should get going. I have to be to work soon."

"What do you do? If you don't mind me asking. It's just, that's kind of a late start, is all," he said. Was he nervous?

"Oh, I'm a court reporter and spend most of my time at home or in the courtroom. But I help my mom out at her school. Eakwood Elementary. She's the principal."

He nodded. "I see. A court reporter?"

"Yep."

"I'm a lawyer. For Sweeny & Co."

"Oh, wow. Interesting."

"What company do you work for?"

I told him, and we chatted a bit longer about our respective positions. My company worked with a large amount of law firms, but Sweeny & Co. wasn't on our list, to my knowledge. Too bad.

"I'm so sorry for taking up so much of your time. I know you said you had to get going. I can be a bit—enthusiastic—when it comes to my work," he apologized, reaching down to pet Clem.

"Not a problem. It was great to chat with you. We have a lot in common." Geez, did that sound like a pick-up line?

"Well, enjoy your walk. And your day."

"Same to you." I continued on my way, feeling a little euphoric as Clem and I trundled along. I didn't even feel the chilly wind on my face. I couldn't stop smiling. We had a connection. I knew it.

* * *

"Prue, dear. How are you this morning?"

"Hi, Mom." I stepped into Mom's office, where she was seated behind her desk. "How are you?"

"I do believe I asked you first."

I smiled, shaking my head. "My morning has been fine. Nothing out of the ordinary." Except finally having a real conversation with a very hot man. No biggie. "And you?"

"The usual craziness around here. Beware—I think the flu bug is going around. We've already sent two kids home and it's not even lunchtime."

I wrinkled my nose. "Already? It seems early for that."

Mom shrugged her narrow shoulders. "It is what it is. How was watching the game on Sunday? You were with Linds, correct?"

I chatted with Mom a while longer, until I had to get hustling to the lunchroom. I passed the second grade class as I was going in, as they were lined up along the wall waiting to get the go-ahead from Sue, who would take their lunch numbers and import what they were having into the computer system.

Maisy gave me an enthusiastic hello and I asked her about her weekend, which set her off into a tizzy of activities that she did with her children. I listened to her chatter on about carpooling, dance classes, soccer games. I felt a small twinge. I thought Deacon and I would be married soon and then well on our way to having children. Now, I was stalled. Who knew when I would get married, much less be ready for children? I had to start all over, completely from scratch. I had to date, meet a man's family, get to know his baggage—and him mine—because in your late twenties, you typically have at least one bag with you.

Then all the dating, the proposal, the engagement

period, the wedding. Having a decent amount of years under our married belt before we decide we're ready for kids. I was twenty-seven, and if I added at least three years of dating, plus another for the engagement . . . Oh my God. Would I ever have children?

"And how was your weekend?" Maisy asked, snapping me out of my trance.

"What? Oh, okay. Just a lot of work and I watched the Bears game yesterday with a friend." How lame, my life compared to hers. Thankfully, the kids came in then, and Maisy and I set to work, making sure they got their trays, the right amount of food, got seated, and were actually eating versus just talking. Each class got twenty minutes, more like fifteen after they got their food and were seated, and the kids needed all that time to actually eat their food.

"Miss Prue! Miss Prue!" One little brunette girl, Ana, called me over to her. I stepped up to her table, overwhelmed by the scent of chicken strips and mashed potatoes. My stomach growled, clearly angry I didn't feed it enough food this morning.

"Yes, Miss Ana?" I asked when I got to her.

"Guess what I did this weekend?"

I crouched down so I was on her level. "What?"

As she launched into her story of cheerleading camp and how she got to be on the top of the pyramid, I smiled at her excited chatter. Every day I was here she told me about her previous evening or what her plans for that night were. I usually had to cut her off and remind her to eat or else she would probably talk the entire time.

"Sounds like you had a fun time! All right, get to eating those chicken strips. Almost time for recess!" I stepped away and a little boy, Derek, waved his hand at me.

Walking over to him, he spooned a big heap of mashed potatoes in his mouth and grinned at me, the mashed vegetable oozing between the missing spaces in his mouth.

"Derek! Eat your food, silly. Those aren't good lunch room manners," I reminded him, but I was smiling and patted his shoulder as I walked by.

I tried to ignore the note of panic that wanted to rise after my earlier thoughts. I had to believe it would work out for me in the end. I deserved it.

Chapter 7

NELLIE

Friday afternoon. I checked Prue Doherty in like usual, watched her grab a towel and head to her room, and soon caught notice on the screen that her bed was on and running. Fifteen minutes later, she shuffled up to the front, wiping tears from her eyes.

"Prue?" I said softly, still surprising myself that I was actually doing this. Why was I doing this?

She whirled around and looked at me, the look of surprise on her face probably matching my own.

"Yes? Is there a problem?" she asked, looking concerned. I was assuming she meant with her account, so I moved to assure her.

"No, no problem. I just—I just wanted to ask if you were okay. I know it's none of my business," I hurried on when she took a breath, "I've just noticed you seem upset when you come in here and I wanted to reach out to you. I'm Nellie, by the way. Nellie Hawthorne. I own the business." I smiled and moved to offer her my hand, coming out from the behind the counter to seem more personable.

She still looked surprised, but shook my hand. "I'm Prue. Prue Doherty. But you know that, I guess." She let out a little laugh, and I smiled, as if to encourage her. "Thank you for taking the time to say something. That's very kind of you."

"I just thought I would do a quick check in on one of my regular clients. I know it's none of my business, but I—I —well, I honestly don't really know what I thought I could do. But I just wanted to say something." Well, that was at least honest.

She gave me a small smile. "Well, I feel pretty silly knowing that I've been caught crying each week. I thought I hid it pretty well."

I smiled back. "I know it's none of my business," I repeated, "but I really hope whatever it is you're going through that you get passed it soon. Or if it's not that easy to get over, that you at least start to be able to move on."

She looked at me, thoughtfully. "You know, it will sound so silly if I tell you what's really going on. Geez, I feel silly even just saying it in my head."

I smiled but didn't say anything. Was she really going to tell me? That would be a little surprising, considering I was a stranger.

"My boyfriend left me. And sure, that's not the end of the world, but it's the whole situation. We had just bought a house, and I'm still paying the mortgage even though I moved out after finding out he was sleeping with a co-worker of ours. We—the three of us—all worked at the same company. I lost my boyfriend—who I thought would be proposing any day—and a friend of mine all in one day. And my house. And a lot of my savings account. But at least I got to keep the dog. That's something, right?" She laughed, a little harshly.

Shit. That did sound bad. "Wow. I'm really sorry to hear that, Prue. What a . . . situation." I almost said "fucked-up" then realized I probably shouldn't be dropping F-bombs around clients, no matter what the situation called for.

"Yeah. I'm trying to move on, really, but it's hard when I'm blowing thousands on a mortgage, racking up lawyer bills because I have to take him to court, and living in a cramped apartment with a seventy-pound yellow Labrador that is meant for a house, not a foot of grass outside my deck door."

I felt like my eyebrows were in my hairline, yet . . . I couldn't help but be a little fascinated. This total stranger was now giving me her life story just because I tried to be nice, but I couldn't help finding her issues to be kind of silly. I mean, really—I get heartbreak sucks and all that shit, but come on. Learn what living a hard life is really like and then we can chat. But, I tried for empathy.

She was still going. "I mean, I'm lucky because I don't have to go into the office every day and see them together. And I'm starting to talk to a guy. I mean, not really. Just on our walks. But perhaps he could turn out to be someone. My friend Linds says I need to get out there and get a rebound guy, but that's not really who I am, you know?"

She looked at me expectedly, and I nearly had to shake my head at her babble. What? Rebound guy? She didn't have one yet? What the hell was she doing then? Going through vibrators on a daily basis?

"Huh," I said, realizing I had to say something to all that chatter. "I just—wow. That's so hard to wrap my mind around." Well, that was the truth.

"I'm so sorry. I can't believe I just went off like that. That's not who I usually am, I swear. Clearly, this . . . situation has me a little crazy."

"Understandable."

"This might sound really weird, but would you like to grab coffee sometime? Not so I can unload more of my problems, I promise. I just—I think I need to get out of my apartment, keep my mind focused on other things. It might be nice to make a new . . . friend. If that isn't super forward and this isn't totally freaking you out."

It totally was. "Not at all!" I said, putting a hand on her shoulder in an attempt to look more sincere. But what the hell? I needed a distraction right now. With Calvin suddenly back in my life and Harrison not relenting about baby shit, this could be good for me.

"What are you doing Monday morning?" I asked, steering her to the door. "Coffee, say eight o'clock?"

* * *

"Nellie, we need to talk."

My hand froze while reaching for my GlamGlo mud mask. I was in the master bathroom, getting ready to give myself a spa night to relax after a crazy week. Face mask was about to be applied, the bath was running and scented with bath bombs, and I was going to apply a deep-conditioning hair mask on my limp strands once I was done lolling about in the tub.

But the tone in my husband's voice stopped me cold. Something was really wrong. Had he found out about Calvin? My abortions? The drugs from my past? There were too many stories he could find out about me. I knew they would catch up to me sometime.

"What is it?" I tried to keep my tone light, not meeting his eyes when he came in the bathroom and stood behind me.

"My mom called me today."

Oh shit. Mrs. Hawthorne knew? How? I bet she hired a fucking private detective to finally break into my past. I knew she was capable of doing it. I tried my hardest to stay on her good side, but I knew she could see through me.

"Oh yeah?"

"Two more of her friends' daughters announced their pregnancies."

Huh? That was not what I was expecting to come out of his mouth.

"She's upset, Nellie." He leaned against the granite countertop and rubbed a hand over his face. "She wants grandchildren, and I'm her only hope. I had to listen to her go on for an hour about how we need to reproduce, and soon. She was really upset."

I felt my entire body nearly sag with relief. That was all? Thank fucking Jesus.

"So? Harrison, come on. Having a baby is a personal decision, and one that your mother should not be involved in."

"You know how she is," he said, as I dipped my fingers into the jar and began to rub the mixture on my face. "She's a part of everything. And she really is upset. And starting to get worried. She kept asking me if we were both able to have children and that perhaps we should get checked out."

My fingers paused for just a moment before I got to spreading the gooey mask around. "And did you tell her nothing is wrong with us, we just haven't started trying yet?"

"Not exactly."

This new tone in his voice had me locking eyes with him. "Harrison. What did you tell her?"

"I might have told her we were trying. For only a few months," he hurried on once seeing my face. "I told her it wasn't a big deal but she insisted we get some testing done." I could tell he could see my ears were probably turning red (along with my face, though that was now turning gray thanks to the mask) and he continued. "But she scheduled appointments for us both, not just you or anything. She's not trying to blame you or anything like that."

Which meant she was. "You really think we should go ahead with these appointments? They're a waste of time. I'm sure we're fine, but who knows until we actually start trying for these magical children?" I said, completing my task of applying the facial mask.

"I mean, I don't think it's a terrible idea or anything."

I rolled my eyes. "Harrison, come on. Why would there be anything wrong with us?" My heart was beating so fast it hurt. If we went to appointments that his mother set up, she would find a way to get the results, no matter what confidentiality or HIPPA bullshit offices pulled. She would know. She would know about the abortions, the complications, the scarring, the infertility. She would know I knew all this before I married her precious only son and kept that information from him. And by association, her. I was fucked. We could not go through with these appointments.

"Well, I think it's completely inappropriate. I don't feel the need to waste my time or money on these frivolous appointments. If we start trying and nothing happens, sure. But until then, why bother?"

"So you want to start trying?"

"Where did you get that from?" I snapped, beyond exasperated.

"You just said . . ." He trailed off, looking confused.

I let out a deep breath. "Harrison, honey, I'm going to take a bath now. I can't keep talking much longer with this sh—stuff—on my face. It hardens and I don't want it to crack yet. Please tell your mother we say no thank you to her appointments at this time. And let me actually consider this baby thing. You barely gave me a chance to breathe, much less actually consider having a baby, carrying a child, and changing my entire life. Our entire life."

He looked like he wanted to say more, and I held up my hand. "I can't talk anymore. I'm taking a bath. I'll be out in a while."

And with that, I removed my robe, naked underneath, and slid under the warm film of bubbly water, not bothering to look back at my husband.

Fertility appointments. Well, fuck me.

Chapter 8

PRUE

I felt silly caring so much about what I wore on Monday morning. It was just coffee. But with Nellie Hawthorne. What was I doing? Had I finally lost my mind? No. I was just making a new friend. Maybe she needed a friend herself. Or maybe this would be a one-time thing. That's what I was hoping for. Just to understand her and then move on. Right?

And I could admit to myself that I was looking forward to some social time, even though this wasn't completely on the up-and-up. I somehow turned in to one of those girls that let my boyfriend rule my life. I hung out with him nearly twenty-four-seven, especially after we moved in together. I went out with his friends and didn't bother to try to make lasting friendships with his friends' girlfriends, mostly because they just rotated every few months or so, and after losing these new "friends" so often because of their breakups, I just got tired of getting close with anyone.

I talked to Maisy and a few other teachers at Mom's school, but nothing of substance. Outside of the usual: how was your weekend, can you believe the Cubs are going to the playoffs, oh good another losing year for the Bears, that was about the extent of our conversations. Linds was really my only true friend, but since moving out to Oamark Park and not seeing her in the office every day, our friendship was changing.

So, I was doing something about that. And so much more. No more shy little Prue always getting burned and hurt. I was finally making a change. It had been years in the making. Years of being bullied and taken advantage of and wrongly accused, and I sat back and took it. No more. I was done.

After deciding to dress in simple black leggings and a burgundy long-sleeved top, paired with brown boots with a chunky heel to give me a little bit of height and a black and white scarf, I thought I looked good for coffee and the outfit would still be fine—if just a little on the dressy side—for when I had to head to school. And then after I was done there, I had to make my way to Chicago, as I needed to go into the office for some prep work on an upcoming deposition I was scheduled for. It promised to take up a lot of my time the next few weeks, and I needed to make sure I was prepared.

I made sure to take Clemmie on an extra-long walk in the morning because I knew I wouldn't get home until late at night. I felt guilty for leaving her alone for so long, but

Mom said she would drop by after dinnertime and let her outside and maybe even take her for a walk around the block, so I felt a little better. Still, I gave her bowl of carrots and green beans (she loved them) to nosh on while I continued to get ready, then after one more trip outside, she obediently went into her kennel and I was out the door.

I tried to give myself a pep talk before walking to the Bean Queen. Don't come across as desperate. Don't talk too much about Deacon. Ask Nellie questions about herself. Don't dominate the conversation. Don't be a Debbie downer. Don't seem too interested in her marriage.

I stood in line and ordered a white mocha latte and a scone, taking my breakfast and finding a table for two in the small dining area. I set my purse on the ground beside me, took out my Kindle, and started to read while I waited, trying to calm my nerves. I couldn't believe I was really going through with this. The change was officially happening. It wasn't long before I heard a voice beside me.

"Prue?"

I looked up to see Nellie standing there, coffee cup in hand, already stained with her lipstick marks.

"Nellie. Hi. I'm glad you could come."

She smiled and took the seat across from me. "Good morning."

"Good morning." I cleared my throat awkwardly. "This is kind of weird, right?"

She laughed, causing me to join in. "A little. But that's okay. As long as we both agree, I guess."

My lips curved up, and I felt some of the tension leave my body. "I really didn't mean to come off quite so— strange at your store. It's just . . . I guess when I get to lie

95

there by myself for ten minutes with nothing to do but think, it starts to stir up a lot of emotions."

"I can completely understand. And trust me—I've owned the shop for over two years now, and I see and hear a lot of things. It doesn't take much to surprise me these days."

The tension came back. She seemed like a nice person. She seemed genuine at first glance. That wasn't a part of the plan.

"But don't worry, I don't want to sit here and talk about my woe is me situation." I forced myself to continue to talk, though my palms were starting to feel damp. It was hard being this kind of person. And did she look almost a little disappointed when I said that?

"That's not a problem either, Prue. If you need someone to talk to—someone neutral, perhaps—I can be that person. And because you're a client at my store, I want you to know I respect that. Well, I would even if you weren't a client, but still. Whatever you have to say it will be confidential. It would stay between us."

I glanced at her left hand, for the first time noticing the large diamond ring and sparkling wedding band underneath it. Sheesh. That thing was huge.

She followed my eyes. "I don't even need to tell my husband about it. Lately, it seems like we don't talk much anyway. We're both so busy running our own lives."

That piqued my interest. "Really? That sounds . . . sad."

She shrugged, looking down at her cherry-lipstick-rimmed coffee cup. "He's a busy guy. I'm busy too, but, you know. We're just busy."

"Too busy for each other?"

She shrugged again, not saying anything.

"How long have you been married for?"

"Almost three years."

I nodded, thoughts racing. Only three years and they were already done talking to each other? Interesting.

"I'm sorry. That's . . . a bummer."

She gave a grim smile. "Yeah. A bummer."

We sat in silence for a few more moments, and I tried to think of something to say. Would it be weird if I kept asking about her marriage? Probably.

"Do you have any pets?" I finally blurted out.

She looked up at me, seeming a little surprised. "Pets? No. Between our work schedules, we wouldn't have time to take care of anything."

I nodded, a little sad. Pets were great. Clemmie was everything to me. Unconditional love, every single day.

"You have a dog, right?" she asked, and at first I was confused. How could she have known that? Then I remembered my rambling after tanning and saying I at least got to keep the dog.

"Yep. Clementine. Or Clemmie. Or Clem. She's a yellow Lab." I reached for my cell phone and showed her my background, Clemmie's big face filling the screen, her long tongue hanging out of her mouth.

Nellie smiled. "Cute dog."

"Thanks." I set my phone back on the counter. "She really is my best friend. Deacon—my ex—didn't seem to have much interest in keeping her, even though he was basically the one to talk me into getting her. Our house didn't even have a fence yet when we first moved in, and I thought we should wait but he insisted. But once we got her, I absolutely fell in love. When everything . . . fell apart . . . I knew I had to have her. And he barely put up a fight about it."

"Well, I would hope not after what he did! You deserved the dog."

I tried to smile. "Thanks. She really does help me out every day. Keeps me from getting too lonely. Keeps me active. Gets me outside. I can't imagine life without her."

"That's sweet."

We drank our coffees quietly again, and I couldn't think of anything else to say.

Nellie opened the conversation this time, asking me a question about the tanning salon and what brought me in there. We chatted easily for the next ten minutes about non-personal topics, which was nice. Much more carefree. My breath came easier. I was really pulling this off. Look at me now.

I glanced at my watch at one point, catching the time. "Oh shoot! I have to get going. I have to be to work in fifteen minutes."

Nellie looked at her own Michael Kors timepiece around her slim wrist. "I should get going as well. It was really nice having this chat with you, Prue."

"You as well." I held my breath. I didn't feel as . . . satisfied as I had hoped I might after our meet up today. Did I dare ask for another coffee date?

"Maybe we could do it again sometime? I have some . . . free time coming up in my schedule," she went on, slinging her purse over her shoulder and looking at me.

I felt relieved. I couldn't feel guilty if she was the one

asking. Right? "Sure thing. After next week, my schedule might get a little more hectic, so what about Wednesday? Maybe after I come in we could grab a late lunch or something?"

She looked thoughtful for a moment, then nodded. "Wednesday. Lunch it is."

NELLIE

High School

Somehow, I made it to high school. I put a lot of credit into the books I read. I was able to escape my shitty life long enough to make believe I was in another one and forget about all the terrible things that were happening. Sometimes I even pretended to be the characters I was reading about. I told people I was diabetic or that I was a part of a shipwreck and was stuck on an island for days before rescue. I made up living in California with my dad and spending a holiday at a haunted house. It was better than telling the truth.

Upon entering high school, I got the stupid idea to try out for cheerleading. In the books I read, the popular girls were always the cheerleaders or the dancers. It was some harebrained scheme that perhaps if I could completely change who I was that I would be accepted by more people, thus somehow turning my life around. Like I said, fucking harebrained.

Somehow, I made it through tryouts and on to the team. To say I was shocked was an understatement. I actually had rhythm somehow and could easily remember the steps and moves and punches and kicks. Prancing was new to me and that took a bit of trying and feeling completely ridiculous, but I did it. I earned a pair of pom-poms.

I really tried turning my shit around once I made the squad. Just two weeks into school and I had already gained somewhat of a reputation—easy with the guys, tough with

101

the girls. I was in three fights during the first week, one at school and two near the public bus stop where I would take the transportation to and from our new trailer each morning and afternoon. I didn't let anyone push me around, and that included older seniors that thought they could run their mouths around me.

But after I saw my name posted to that piece of paper, I made a real effort. Especially when one of the varsity cheerleaders pulled me aside after my science class and informed me that now I was a part of the squad, outfits like the one I was wearing were not considered appropriate. I looked down at my leather black miniskirt and chunky heels.

That night, I took the bus to the local mall and stole a bag of clothes from a junior's store that I figured were more "appropriate."

I quickly befriended Jemima, a sophomore. She was a bubbly, short little thing, with dirty blonde hair always in a ponytail and a big red ribbon to accentuate her cheerleader status. She was a little on the thick side and was so strong, which made her the perfect base for our stunts. She always offered to be my base—since I was smaller, they chose me to be a flyer—and she helped walk me through any cheer routines that I struggled with.

Within the first month of school, our cheer coach Darlene announced that two freshman cheerleaders would be chosen to move up to the varsity squad. She explained this was standard practice, in order to help groom those girls to one day be the leaders of the varsity squad after the older girls graduated. Jemima took me under her wing after that announcement and helped me not only practice longer and harder, but continue to dress the part (out were my miniskirts, in were khakis) and study to make sure my grades stayed up, a requirement for any student athlete.

When the day of the big announcement came, I thought I was going to be sick with nerves. I knew I had given it my all, and with someone like Jemima on my side (she had moved up to varsity the year prior), I thought I had a pretty good chance.

Jemima was the one who called my name as making it to the varsity squad. I cried with happiness as the other girls hugged me in congratulations. I felt . . . a part of something. Included. Happy, for the first time in so long.

Jemima became my new best friend, having her older boyfriend pick me up in the morning so we could drive to school together and her parents drove me home. We sat together on the bus for away games and she would braid my hair. I quit drugs and smoking cold turkey, and even gave up guys during those months. I was doing bigger things with my life. I wasn't going to turn into my mother. Jemima and the other cheerleaders were changing me.

And then . . . it all came crashing down. Jemima's boyfriend came on to me at the Fall Formal dance in late October. I was coming out of the bathroom by myself and he was waiting for me. He grabbed me around the waist and pushed me up against the wall, trying to kiss me. I had turned my head, trying to push him off me. What the hell was he doing? I would never do that to my best friend.

"Come on, slut. I've heard you do it all. Don't try to give me this prissy shit. You're not like Jesus Jemima. You know you want it."

I was just bringing my knee up to get him in the dick

when Jemima and two other cheerleaders turned the corner and saw us. He pulled back and said I had come on to him, and I tried to defend myself but to no avail. I was left stranded at the dance that night, as I was supposed to go to Jemima's for an after-party. She would have nothing to do with me.

I ended up going home with her boyfriend that night and getting high with him in his shitty RAV4 and didn't even fight it when he requested anal sex. It wasn't my favorite, but what the fuck ever. My life was already ruined. Might as well feel like the whore I knew I was. Three months of pretending to be someone different. And that's all it was. Pretend.

Darlene called me into the office on Monday during school hours. She said Jemima and her mother had called her over the weekend and explained the situation, and then handed me an envelope. My fate was sealed. Jemima's boyfriend had also taken explicit pictures of us—well, just me, his face was hidden from view in each one—from the weekend and was apparently passing them around the school. No wonder I was getting all the looks and leers today. I had figured Jemima told people that I tried to get on her boyfriend, not that everyone now knew what my tits looked like and the explicit photos of a dick in my ass.

I was off the squad and kicked out of school that day. And the downward spiral continued.

PRUE

17 Years Ago

In sixth grade, I was a shy little girl. I didn't have an easy time making friends because I was so quiet and reserved. During grades 4-8, Mom, Dad, and I lived on Pine Drive, and a couple months into sixth grade a new family moved in across the street from us. A mom, dad, and three children moved in over the course of a weekend, hauling bags and boxes from multiple trucks inside the house. I watched closely out my bedroom window. Our neighborhood on Pine was really nice and quiet, but all the kids on the block were either much older or much younger than me. I didn't have a friend on the street, so when I saw three new kids moving in, I eyed the prospects eagerly from the living room window.

I first saw a little girl and guessed her to be in the category of much younger than me. I sighed, still watching out the window. Next, I saw a boy in a wheelchair. I frowned at the image. At ten years old, I only knew old people to be in wheelchairs, not what appeared to be a teenage boy being confined to one. Then, I saw her. A skinny girl with long blonde hair and glasses. She was my age, I just knew it. And we would have to be friends. We were neighbors!

On a Sunday evening, my mom, dad, and I walked over to their house, apple pie in hand. We were introduced to the Lawson family. Mom Kathryn Ann, Dad Douglas,

Joey was the brother in the wheelchair, Clara the little girl, and Tina was my age and enrolling in my middle school. The grown-ups talked to one another for a while about boring grown-up stuff, while Tina showed me her room. She collected bugs, like ants and beetles, which I thought was kind of weird. We didn't become best friends that night, and our trio walked home about an hour later, me feeling dejected.

Tina's first day at school, I could tell she felt awkward and uncomfortable. Even though I knew we weren't going to be close friends, I tried to help her out. I showed her around the cafeteria, where to change in gym class, and warned her about not sitting next to Nick Slater, whose bad breath was legendary. As the weeks passed, Tina and I actually did turn out to be somewhat close friends. Even though I still thought she was a little weird because of how much she knew and talked about creepy crawlies, I still liked her company.

I got to know her little sister, an energetic ball of blonde hair and chubby legs, who was starting kindergarten in the elementary school the following year. I found out her brother Joey had been in a car accident in the town they previously lived in. His friends' parents were driving Joey and his friend back from the park and were blindsided by a drunk driver at six o'clock on a Sunday night. Everyone in the car died at the scene, but miraculously, Joey was still alive, yet paralyzed from his chest down. The family made the decision to move for a fresh start and leave behind the terribly sad memories.

I felt so bad for Tina when she told me the story with tears in her eyes. I can still remember trying to think of how one accident could take so many lives and how overwhelming that made me feel, even as just a young girl. It made me go home and hug my parents, who were already aware of the situation. While I still didn't think we would ever be best friends like the girls I would see on the Disney TV shows, Tina and I still formed a nice friendship.

At our school, even only in sixth grade, we still had our own version of the "cool girls." The clique consisted of Berkley, Morgan, Allison, and Heather. They were rude to others, always thinking they were better than anyone else, and downright disrespectful—to students and teachers as well. They were constantly in trouble or causing trouble, yet, all the girls wanted to be their friends still. I was included in that camp, and back then I had no idea why I wanted their acceptance so badly.

One winter day, with about a foot of snow on the ground, we were at our only outdoor recess of the day. Everyone had snow pants, boots, hats, and mittens, so no part of our bodies was showing. We still went outside for recess unless the temperature was below zero, so even though it was only nine degrees with a foot of snow, we were outside playing.

As we were walking out of the building, Berkley surprised me by walking beside me. "Hi, Prue," she said, sounding friendly.

"Oh, hi," I said, looking at her with some confusion. Berkley or any of those girls rarely uttered a word to me.

"Want to hang out with us at recess?" she went on to ask, pulling a hat over her dark, shoulder-length thin hair.

I was shocked into silence. I had never been asked to hang out with them—ever. Why did they want me now?

"Yes!" I couldn't say it fast enough. I didn't care why they wanted to hang out with me, just that I wanted to hang out with them. I wanted to be a part of their group. They were so cool and popular. I wanted that too.

I saw Tina was waiting for me in our usual spot when we got outside, but I acted like I didn't see her and followed Berkley to where Morgan, Allison, and Heather were already sitting on the ground, making snow angels and chatting with one another. Everyone said hello to me when I sat down, and no one acted like anything was different from their normal day. I tried to go along with it, all while wondering how soon we would become best friends and if I would finally be invited to their birthday parties. No girls ever were.

Just a few minutes into recess, Allison said, "So, are we ready to go over the plan?"

The other girls and I agreed, and I leaned forward, eager to be in on the plan. I listened in horror as Allison explained who each girl would be targeting. Apparently, their plan was to make a bunch of snowballs and throw them at the "dorks"—the kids who were usually alone at recess. I was already uncomfortable with the plan when Allison gave me my target—Tina.

"What? But she's my friend," I said immediately.

"She's actually your friend?" Morgan asked, looking

disgusted.

"Well, not really. But she's my neighbor." I tried to cover for myself.

"Whatever. Do you have bug girl or not?"

I thought about it for a moment. I thought of what my parents would say if they found out. I thought about Tina's family and what they had been through and my still-new friendship with Tina. I couldn't single her out like that. It would be humiliating for her.

"No. I'm not in," I said firmly.

Berkley huffed. "And we thought you were cool. Bye bye, weirdo. Get out of here."

My eyes burning with tears, I got up and ran away from the mean girls, not believing what had just happened. I was too embarrassed to go by Tina and admit what I had done and what the other girls had said about her and that I had chosen them over her that day, so I just stuck myself in a slide the rest of recess and cried until it was time to go in.

The next day at recess, I noticed Tina walking out with Allison. My eyes narrowed. Were they trying to get her, too? Thankfully, I knew Tina was a sweet person and would never go along with their types of pranks. I felt relieved knowing I wasn't going to be the only girl to stand up to the bullies.

When Tina's snowball hit me straight in the stomach, with her looking me in the eye, I felt like I would throw up —partly from the hit, and partly from the injustice of it all. I took Tina in when she was new, I made friends with her even though I didn't really want to, and I wouldn't throw a snowball at her just to be a part of the popular crowd. And she turned her back on me so easily. The injustice sickened me. Tina became a part of that mean girl group from that day on, and she happily bullied me throughout the rest of sixth grade. I was too embarrassed to tell my family the nerdy bug girl from across the street had turned into my nemesis, so I let it continue until Tina's family moved away again, after finding a better school to accommodate Joey's lifestyle. Middle school was not a pleasant time for me, and I continue to get upset to this day when I recall the torture little Tina inflicted on me.

Chapter 9

NELLIE

Over the next week, I had lunch and then a coffee date with Prue. It was weird, but she was kind of . . . refreshing. She was naïve as fuck, but refreshing. She clearly needed a friend. And I needed . . . a distraction. I needed Harrison to stop bugging me about having kids, and I needed to forget that my past fling was now living in my small suburb.

It was obvious that she liked when I talked about my relationship with Harrison. She wanted to know that not every relationship out there was a bed of roses. She apparently had been burned pretty bad by her ex and that co-worker, so if she needed to hear that marriage wasn't all that and a bag of chips, so be it. And I didn't mind chatting with her about a lot of our issues, but I kept the obvious ones under wraps—who I really was, that whole infertility business. She didn't really press me for a lot of information, but somehow it seemed to come out of me. She was so open and friendly and just nice. And she really just wanted to . . . talk.

On Friday morning, we were back at the Bean Queen, drinking coffees, and she was eating a scone, no breakfast for me besides the java. Too many carbs with everything that they sold in this place. Prue was in the midst of telling me how she fell for Deacon.

"He's in IT, and he started working for the company we're at now about six months after we started dating. We met via mutual friends, and I thought it was sweet he wanted to eventually work with me and spend more time with me. I mean, that wasn't his only reason of course, but some couples wouldn't want to work together, and he liked the idea. I honestly thought it was love at first. And he would tell me that too. That he thought it was love at first sight."

I held back from rolling my eyes. Love at first sight was the biggest line of bullshit ever. Lust, yes. Intense need to fuck someone? Sure. But love? No way. And working together so they didn't have to be apart? Gag me.

I nodded and took another drink. "That is so sweet."

She sighed wistfully, like something out of a sappy movie or something. "I know. And we were so happy in the beginning. It was like something out of a romantic movie."

Her words mirrored my thoughts. Weird. "So what happened?" I'll admit, her story did have me curious. He sounded like the perfect dude. And she the perfect girl. But not everything was always how it seems . . . trust me. I was an expert at proving that.

"And then one day I caught them. And it was over."

"But caught them how? Where?" She winced, and I tried to backtrack so I didn't sound like a Jerry Springer enthusiast. "I'm sorry, that was really inconsiderate of me. But I'm just so confused. Deacon sounded so great. And Brandi was a friend-ish of yours. Why would they do it?"

She shrugged, looking at a spot on the wall behind me. "I wish I knew. I caught them at our house. The darn house we had just moved into. I didn't even have the house décor finalized yet and he was in our bedroom with her."

I tried to imagine the scene. A new house, boxes still everywhere. No homey feel to it because Prue didn't have the "décor" settled on yet. And a guy and girl illicitly tangled in the sheets, selfish to the point of betrayal of their other half, and a friend. Damn.

"And you never had any idea? How long had they . . . been together for?"

"Deacon said it had been six months."

I arched a brow. "So he was with her when you bought your house? And the dog?"

She nodded, looking down at the table. "Yep. I mean —why even bother? It's hard and complicated and time-consuming to buy a house. Why go through all that when you know you don't even want to be with the person you're buying it with?"

"Do you think he was going to leave Brandi at some point and be faithful to you again?"

"I don't know. Honestly. Why would he if he could have us both? But would Brandi have wanted something more eventually and told him to leave me? He says he was going to leave her and he promised he wasn't unfaithful in our relationship other than that, but I don't know how to believe him."

I nodded thoughtfully, processing her words. "Did you know he was cheating?"

"What?" She looked confused.

"Did you know? Or not know, I guess, but have a feeling? Or did your mom or your friends? Usually someone has some idea that something funny is going on."

Her eyes flickered. "If I knew, why would I stay with him?"

I frowned. "I don't know. I guess you wouldn't. I just hear stuff about gut instincts and women's intuition." Her mouth turned down, so I tried to hurry on and once again cover my tracks. "I never really believed in that stuff, though. It just seemed like a question to ask."

She gave me a tight smile. "Not to worry. But no. I didn't."

Something in the air had shifted. She was lying. Trust me—a chronic liar knows when someone was lying. Why did she stay with Deacon if she knew he was cheating? Why would she buy the house? Essentially, she had a hand in all this drama she was going through. Even if she had a slight suspicion he was cheating, she shouldn't have gone through with purchasing a house with him. What was her real story? And how soon could I uncover it?

I looked down at my watch. "I should get going. We open soon."

She looked relieved. "Okay. I hope you have a good weekend."

"Are you not coming in today?" It wasn't her regular day, but I just assumed since we were meeting she would follow me to the salon.

"Not today." She smiled. "I think I can cut back on the sessions. I'm feeling a lot better lately. Time heals all wounds and all that. And . . . talking to you I think helps, too. And my mom says I'm getting a little too tan for her liking. Good thing I'm not a selfie queen or anything." She laughed.

I smiled back, but I felt a little panicked. We hadn't exchanged phone numbers or any other personal info. I figured we would set up at least one weekend date while she was in today. "Well, I hate to lose a customer of course, but I'm so happy we're connecting. Do you have a busy weekend?"

She stood up from the table, clearly not needing to be anywhere that day judging by her running pants and tennis shoes. "Not really. Probably just hanging out with Clemmie and my mom at some point."

I thought through Harrison's schedule. He told me he was doing something this weekend . . .

"Are you a football fan?" I asked, remembering he was having some guys over on Sunday. While I didn't mind having a house full of guys swearing at the television set and leaving a mess of my kitchen, I knew Harrison would participate heartily in beer drinking with said guys, and be horny afterward, and then try to talk babies with me again.

"Like the NFL? Yeah, I watch the Bears and keep up with their season. You?"

Interesting. "Not really. My husband is having friends over on Sunday, so I was thinking about doing something better with my time."

"Like what?"

My mind raced. Where would be a safe place that we

would have no chance to run into Calvin? I hated I had to keep thinking like this. "Mani/pedi?"

She looked thoughtful for a moment, then nodded. "I don't usually splurge on that kind of stuff with the whole money situation, but I'd be up for that."

"Hey, great. How about an early dinner Sunday then the spa? I'll call my usual gal and make the reservation."

She looked a little surprised, but judging by her bare nails and wicked cuticles, she wasn't a regular of manicures, of the spa or DIY-variety. "Sounds good."

And hopefully I could stretch it so Harrison would either be passed out or too tired to come after me with babies on the brain.

"Perfect."

Chapter 10

PRUE

My heart was beating like crazy when I left Bean Queen and made the jog home. In my haste to get away from that awkward conversation, I had forgotten to put my hat on, and the cold wind in my ears quickly made me grab that out from my sweatshirt pocket and slip it on, pulling it tight around my ears, which were now burning.

I didn't know Deacon was cheating with Brandi. I didn't know he was cheating . . . for sure. Did I have an idea, an inkling, an intuition? Maybe.

I don't know how many months it was. No. That was a lie. My feet pounded the pavement, wanting to get home and explore this more. I thought I would never open that bag of worms, but Nellie had my mind racing.

I got home five minutes quicker than I had last time, according to the pedometer app on my iPhone. I couldn't just get to what I wanted to do, though. Not with Clemmie whining in her kennel. Being a pet owner was hard work and unselfish, but I did love it.

I clipped Clem to her leash and we did a quick jaunt outside. She clearly didn't appreciate the cooler weather today either—or she picked up on my anxiousness to get inside—and quickly did her business and moved toward the door.

"Good girl, boos," I said as we trooped inside, and I gave her a full carrot to chew on while I searched the closet in the bedroom.

She padded along behind me as we made our way down the single short hallway in the apartment, and lay on the floor to chew her carrot while I pushed aside clothes, shoes, shoe boxes, winter boots, and so much more. I finally came across a small clear tote, rectangular and with a white plastic lid keeping everything sealed inside.

I took the tote over to my bed, sitting on top of the perfectly made sheets and fluffy cream comforter. I had bought myself a whole bed set upon moving out. No, this wasn't the bed that I caught Deacon and Brandi in. I let him keep that California king that he had insisted on buying when we first moved into our condo together, even though moving a bed that big into a small condo on the 17th floor of a building was the biggest pain known to man.

No, this was my queen bed that fit Clemmie and me perfectly, that used to be our bed before the king invaded our bedroom and the queen was moved to storage, then our spare bedroom in the new house for a few weeks until I moved out.

I went on a bit of a shopping binge after everything

happened. New bed set, new coffee tables, new clothes, new kitchen table. I left Deacon with a lot of our stuff because I'd been too upset to think logically—or fairly—and he obviously wasn't a decent enough person to offer it up. Once I realized just how precarious my financial situation was going to be, I felt like a grade-A fool. Another reason when my mom came a-calling for help at the school that I pitched in without many second thoughts.

I looked at Clemmie lying on the floor, still happily eating her carrot, then back to the tote. I swung my legs off the bed and sat next to my dog, running a hand through her silky hair. I needed moral support to do this.

She looked at me with her big brown eyes and I think gave me a nod. Or she twitched. Regardless, I took a breath and took the lid off. Obviously, it was a Deacon box. I wasn't one of those girls to fly into a fit of rage when dealing with conflict and burn and shred my memories. Instead, as I was frantically moving out of "our" new house, I shoved everything into this tote, and hadn't opened it up until now. I just wasn't ready yet.

But something Nellie said was bothering me. I guess maybe it was time for me to admit to myself that my relationship with Deacon wasn't perfect, like maybe I tried to paint it to some people. Obviously no relationship was, and perhaps sometimes I tried to go overboard with how happy and in love we were. I didn't lie, I simply . . . over exaggerated. It wasn't like Deacon was abusive or we didn't talk to each other when were home or didn't touch one other or called each other names. Nothing like that. But maybe it wasn't quite the Hallmark movie I portrayed it to be.

I rifled through the photos quickly. The first holiday party where Deacon asked me out. Our first Christmas together. Vacations. Celebrating milestones together.

Because I'm one of "those girls," I also had movie stubs in the box, game tickets to our first Cubs outing, a rock from the spot where we had our first picnic. I rubbed the smooth stone between my thumb and forefinger, remembering that day vividly, as it was also our first time being together, together. We'd had a romantic picnic followed by a hike, then went back to his place after picking up hot fudge sundaes from the ice cream parlor down the street from him and made love. I remembered him tasting like chocolate that night and suddenly swiped at a tear that I felt streaming down my face, not even realizing when I had started crying.

Clemmie suddenly whined and placed her head in my lap, huffing out a breath.

"I know, girl," I said, petting her fur. "I have to get it together."

I reached for the final item in the tote, the item I had put in there first when I was clearing out my belongings. My journal.

It was nothing fancy, just a non-descript short brown notebook with unlined pages. It was in the same gift package I received at a work holiday party that I didn't put to use until much after receiving it. I didn't plan to journal, just one day I thought I should write down my thoughts. I hid it from Deacon because I obviously didn't want him to read what was inside and figured he would never look in my dresser drawer that was filled with my yoga pants and running shorts.

I thumbed the front cover. There were no words on the front, not My Journal or Dear Diary. I didn't even scribble my name on the front page.

I read through my writing, nothing much of substance for the first few pages. Just how I finally decided I would journal but didn't think I really had anything to say. I was never much of writer—though, I did love reading —so what gave me this idea I wasn't too sure. Perhaps it was my subconscious, alerting me that something wasn't right and that I would one day want to get my feelings out.

October 29

Deacon didn't come home until after two a.m. last night. I stayed up, worried, but didn't want to text him and ask where he was at. I didn't want to be that naggy girl. But where was he for so long? And to come home smelling like a bar? Who was he with? And why didn't he invite me?

November 14

I slept on the couch tonight. We got into a fight because Deacon said he couldn't come to Thanksgiving with Mom and me. When I asked why, he said work was too busy and he just couldn't get out of it. It's not like we have to travel far for the holiday. An hour, maybe two tops when the traffic is terrible. It's Thanksgiving. Family is supposed to be together.

December 12

I think something might be going on with Deacon. He's acting so different. I don't want to believe the worse, but I've started snooping through his things to try to ease my mind. I haven't found anything, but that might be even worse. Because instead, he's deleting everything off his phone. When he was in the shower he left his phone on the charger, and I grabbed it and went to his text messages. Besides the conversation we had the night before and one conversation with Matt from work, there was nothing else there. I know he talks to more people than Matt and me. I even looked at his Snapchat feed and it was completely empty. Since I had just snapped him several times that day, I knew his feed shouldn't be bare and he must have used the Clear All Conversation tools. But why? And who is he talking to?

January 28

Our fighting is getting worse and I don't have anyone to turn to. Mom thinks Deacon is my Prince Charming and Linds, I think, could be more smitten with him than me. And it's my fault. Even when things are bad, I won't admit it to them. But why would I? I don't want them to dislike my boyfriend. I don't want them to think he's a terrible guy, because he's not. Really. He's just a human, but I think I've built him up to be a superhero instead and it's backfiring on me. Hard. I don't have anyone to turn to. Why did I take things to the extreme when it came to our relationship? Why couldn't I have just admitted we have a normal relationship where we fight and don't spend 24-7 in Bliss City? I'm such an idiot.

February 3

I don't think I want to be in this relationship anymore. But it's steamrolling. It's out of my control at this point. Deacon wants to buy a house and I don't know what to do. I don't think I want to be with him anymore. I don't know if he's cheating on me or just doesn't want to be around me, but at least twice a week he doesn't get home until after midnight. At home, we're practically like roommates instead of lovers. I thought we were nearing the end, then suddenly he proposes this house thing on me. Do I say no? How can I let this relationship go, though? I love Deacon. I see forever with him. I just don't know if he sees it with me, and if he doesn't—why the games?

February 28

We're buying a house. I think this is the right decision. So many people would be disappointed if we broke up. I know Mom would be devastated. She wants nothing more than for me to find the right man to settle down with. And she loves Deacon. He's stable, mature, definitely a breadwinner. He likes nice things and has a good family and cooks me dinners. But I fear I'm not in love with him anymore. I think he disrespects me and possibly cheated on me. Or maybe he still is. So why I am still here?

I'm the good girl. I make the right decisions. I'm safe. I'm practical. And Deacon is safe and practical and right . . . I think. But what if I'm making a horrible mistake staying? I'm so confused.

I sat back against the bed, completely spent after reading a few entries. I started sobbing this time, bringing my knees up to my chest. I knew. I knew and I didn't do anything about it. I stayed. I let myself stay in a situation that I knew was wrong. What would I have done if Deacon proposed one day? Would I have let myself get married to someone who I didn't think loved me and who I didn't think I loved back? Was it really so important that I try to be settled down in my mid-twenties that I would go to such lengths to get there? That I had to lie to my friends and even my family about the type of relationship I was in? What was wrong with me?

When did I become the girl that had to have the perfect life? When did I stop caring about being a good, honest person in order to try to achieve that? And what the hell kind of path was I going down now?

Clemmie was licking my face, and I could tell I was scaring my puppy with the terrible noises I was making. I took huge, calming breaths and tried to slow my tears.

I put my head between my knees, alternating stroking Clem and taking a breath. I had to pull it together. I had to get a plan together.

Chapter 11

NELLIE

I have something special planned tonight. Be ready by six. I'll pick you up, and wear something fancy. Love you.

I read the text on my phone and groaned, dropping my head into my hands. Sure, probably any wife would love to get this message, knowing her husband is thinking about her and obviously making lovely plans, but I could see through Harrison. He wanted us to get all fancy, go out on the town, probably consume a few cocktails, then come home and have sex—and make a baby. Not happening, hubby. No way.

I knew I couldn't withhold sex from Harrison forever. That just couldn't happen. And trust me, I didn't want to not be getting laid myself. But if we started having sex on the regular and "trying" to make this Hawthorne heir—without any luck—his mother was going to insist we have those appointments. And then everything would blow up in my face.

I clicked through the schedules in my office, looking over the following week. As expected, appointments were getting a boost. No longer able to go to the beach or sit in the bleachers at Wrigley Field and get a tan, people (women mostly, but men, too) needed to head indoors for their artificial tanning needs. And I wasn't complaining, nor was the staff, especially Kara, who was freelance and worked off appointments only for spray-tan clients.

I closed my eyes and inhaled deeply, trying to think. Could I fake a pregnancy? Well, no. How the hell would I do that? Could I pretend to get pregnant then lose it? That could buy me years before anyone would start hounding us to try again. Right? When it came to my MIL, anything goes, though, so my fake tears probably wouldn't even be dried before she would come calling again.

Damn it. Damn it.

Maybe I could convince a doctor to write a fake report. It could say that I wasn't able to get pregnant because I . . . had something wrong with me. A broken fallopian tube. A blockage on my uterus. (Was that a thing?) Or . . . I sat up straight in my chair. The answer was obvious! It was staring me in the face all along! What I had been trying to hide all these years could turn out to be my get out of jail free card. Why hadn't I thought of this sooner? It was obvious.

"Nellie?" I jumped a little at the sound of Kerri's voice. "Sorry, chica!" she said with a laugh. "Your friend is here. Just wanted to let you know."

"Oh, thanks, Kerri. Sorry, just lost in thought." I

shelved my genius idea away and straightened my blouse, grabbing my Michael Kors bag from next to me. "I'll be right out."

She nodded and walked away, and I looked at the mirror hanging on the wall, grabbing out my ABH lip gloss and giving my already glossy lips another swipe and fluffing up my hair. I felt ten pounds lighter.

I approached the lobby and saw Prue standing there, dressed in jeans and a heavy, baggy sweatshirt. For such a cute girl, she really didn't have much style.

"Prue, hi."

She smiled, her face nearly bare of any makeup. We looked totally different—me, completely done up, hair tamed, nice outfit on, designer bag. But since we were just grabbing lunch on a Wednesday afternoon, it wasn't like she needed to be dressed up. I didn't even really know what she did for a job, besides work with kids at a school or something.

"Hi, Nellie. You look really nice."

"Thanks. These shoes aren't the most comfortable, but I'll survive."

We laughed, and then I called out a farewell to Kerri and Prue and I walked down the sidewalk of the little strip center, just four doors over to a small Mediterranean eatery.

She held open the door for me and I walked inside, taking a few steps to the side to peer at the menu, even though I ate here at least once a week and knew my favorite order. Prue had said she'd never eaten here before, so it was more out of consideration of that.

"What would you recommend?" she asked, peering

up at the blackboard filled with gyros, falafel sandwiches, hummus, and tapas.

"You really can't go wrong here because everything is so fresh, but my favorites are the classic gyro sandwich, the kabob skewers with chicken and vegetables, or the Greek salad. We must also get the baklava for dessert."

She wrinkled her nose, squinting now at the menu. "What is baklava?"

"You've never had baklava? Oh, honey, you haven't lived! It's a delicious dough with walnuts and almonds baked into it, then drizzled with honey syrup. It's my kryptonite, and why I can only let myself eat here once a week. No way can I come here and walk away without getting baklava."

"Okay." She nodded determinedly. "I think I'll get the skewers and the baklava."

"Good choice."

We stepped up to the counter and Eric was already smiling, ready to take our order. He was a nice gentleman, in his late thirties, and his wife was a pediatric surgeon in Chicago. I ate here quite a bit.

"What can I get you ladies?" he asked, and I ordered for both of us, then took out my wallet and said, "One bill, please."

"Oh, Nellie, you don't have to buy my lunch," Prue protested, making to pull her wallet from the sweatshirt pouch.

"It's my treat. I know this is a new place for you, and I just want you to enjoy one of my favorite eateries."

Eric swiped my card and handed it back to me, giving us a wink and then heading off to make our food. We took our drinks and walked over to a small table near a window, settling in to wait for our delicious meal.

"Well, thanks again. That really is nice of you."

I smiled graciously. I did kind of feel like it was the least I could do. I knew she was having money issues and I obviously wasn't. And I felt like perhaps I was forging some sort of . . . friendship with Prue. I mean, not anything of substance. We still really didn't know a lot of details about one another, but it was such a weird situation. I didn't know her favorite color or her mom's name, but I knew about her biggest heartbreak, her money troubles, her desire to find love. She didn't know my husband's name or where my house was, but she knew of my marital troubles. It was kind of bizarre. But we both seemed to understand what the other needed at this time in our lives, and it was just working out.

For some reason, the first five minutes of us meeting each other was always awkward. It was like we wanted to ask how our days were going, how our spouses and family were, but there was no point. While it was unspoken, it was there.

I jumped in first. "So this big case you have coming up. Will you run into Deacon or Brandi while working?"

She took a sip from her soda—not diet, interesting—and let out a sigh. "Brandi, yes. There are three of us assigned to the depo because of how large it is and we physically couldn't be there for all the hours they need us to, plus do all the work that is needed outside of the courtroom. We wouldn't be together in court at the same time and I can do all my notes and proofreading at home and not in the office, but we'll have to be together at some point to exchange notes and feedback. Deacon, thankfully not. Since he's just the IT guy, I don't have to worry about him."

"Well, I guess that's something."

She nodded. "How are things with your husband? Getting any better?"

Eric set our plates in front of us at that moment, and we thanked him. With a tip of his head, he was off.

I stared down at my food. Prue didn't have any association to Harrison, to his family. There was no harm sharing this with her, right? And she might actually be able to give me some feedback or ideas.

"Well, there is a small issue that has come up."

Chapter 12

PRUE

I listened carefully as Nellie described her delicate situation with her husband and how badly he wanted a baby.

"I unfortunately had a lot of complications with my . . . lady parts when I was younger. It was actually recommended that I have a hysterectomy because of the damage to some of them, but I never had the procedure."

"Wow." I pondered that for a moment. "Why didn't you?"

She looked down at her plate of food. "Mostly because of money. I didn't have it for the surgery, I didn't have insurance to cover it, that sort of thing."

"Oh. Yeah, that makes sense."

"Anyway, I . . . I didn't exactly tell him this when we got together. It didn't seem important. I wasn't trying to hide it; it just never came up."

"You guys never had the baby talk?" Deacon and I had the talk, and we were never even engaged.

She looked me right in the eye. "Not really. A few times, short conversations, nothing of substance."

I frowned. "All right. So what's the harm in trying? You never know. If you didn't have the hysterectomy and it's been so many years, maybe something has changed. Maybe try and if it doesn't work see a doctor or something?" I realized I was rambling, rushing out my words.

Her dark eyes seemed to get darker, before she tucked a strand of hair behind her ear, showing off a large diamond earring. "I guess I'm afraid my husband is going to be upset if we can't have children. I'll be upset if we can't have children. Now that I'm older and settled down and I realize how much he wants them, I want them, too. But I don't know what to do. I'm worried he'll be so upset with me. And I'm worried I really won't be able to have them."

I thought this over, trying to think of what I would say to a real girlfriend. "Well, I think you just have to be honest with him. And like you said, it could be all worry for no reason. Maybe you'll try and BAM!" She jumped a little. "Pregnant on the first try."

She gave a faint smile. "Maybe. That sure would be great."

I peered at her, noting her pale face. "You really are worried about this, aren't you?" I couldn't think of what else to say. "I hope it all works out for you," I followed up lamely.

"Thanks, Prue. I think I have a plan, though." She

looked determined, then took another bite of her lunch.

I smiled and took another bite of my skewer, not sure exactly what her plan was, but thinking of my own plan. This new side of me was actually kind of . . . exciting. I'd never played the part of the bad girl, but I thought I was actually doing well in this new role. The new twists and turns I was uncovering, how to turn the information I was receiving to my own benefit. It was slightly thrilling. I didn't know if I should be worried about that or not. But no. I couldn't be. And I enjoyed that a part of my new plan was having Nellie pay for everything. I was going to pinch every penny I could to build my savings account so I could cash in when need be. If Nellie offered to pay, I would gladly accept. That would only help me in the long run. Screw Deacon and Brandi trying to drain me. I would come out on top. For once.

"Are you ready to have your world changed?" she asked then, and I cocked my head.

"How do you mean?"

"The baklava." She pointed at the guy who took our order as he was approaching the table, two little plates in his hands.

"Enjoy, ladies."

"Wow. This looks delicious." I picked up my spoon and put a generous portion on there, sliding it into my mouth. "Whoa."

"I told you." Nellie grinned. "I don't lie."

* * *

After lunch with Nellie, I went home to continue to prep this deposition. Before any big case like this, I got on my steno machine and went through old notes. I'd been a court reporter for ten years, but I still liked to practice. It was like any other job, where you train and practice for the big event. This upcoming case was just that.

I found an old depo that I recorded a few months prior, queued it up on my iPhone and plugged in my headphones. I let my fingers fly over the steno machine, using a three key-stroke to type out "The defendant stated" and a two key-stroke to type "Jury said."

When I first started college for court reporting in Iowa, I was amazed at what these machines could do. It took a lot of hard work and hours and hours of practice to feel like I finally had the hang of it. So many students dropped out of the major because of the intense hours. While my roommates would be going off to parties on Friday nights and not getting home until the wee hours of the morning, I was stuck in my room, practicing key-stroke after stroke, taking notes, transcribing. We were required to do a set amount of hours with our steno machine each day, including on the weekends, so the first year of college was especially brutal when everything was still so foreign.

But I toughed it out, and I was so happy I did. Not only was I able to move back to Chicago and land a job at a top company, but the pay was nothing to scoff at. I was proud of myself for not dropping the major back in my freshman year, even though there were several times I called my mom in tears, wanting to drop out of college and just come home already. She was always able to talk me down from the ledge, and luckily I befriended four other girls in the major, and we would have "practice parties" together and help each other out. Those girls really saved me and made college so much fun.

It was crazy to think that just four years after I graduated, the college stopped offering the major. Even though this career is highly sought out, the enrollment numbers couldn't keep up and too many students were dropping the course for them to keep it alive. It really was just foreshadowing, though, because three years after that, the entire college shut down for good.

I remembered getting a Facebook message from one of my steno friends, Lalani, when the news came out. After the disaster with Amanda, Joelle, and Carli, I was able to move on and form a new group of girlfriends, which would last throughout my college years. Lalani was the only one of us to stay in Iowa; Rose had moved to Nebraska, Steffi to California, and Cate to Alabama. She was going to the farewell party at the school and group messaged all of us to ask if we wanted to come back and go with her. Only Rose had come back for it.

Deacon and I were dating at that time, and though I did mention going back to Iowa for the closing ceremony and party, he had scoffed at the idea. "Eight hours to Des Moines to do what? Go to this boring ceremony and turn around and drive right back? What else would there be to do in Des Moines?"

He said the capital of Iowa like it was a bad word or something. I had been a little miffed that he shot it down so fast. First of all, I really wanted to be a part of that farewell. My college meant a lot to me, and knowing that it was closing its doors for good was really hard to wrap my mind around. But I also could have shown him where I lived, where I partied, where I ate each day on campus. I could have shown him the beautiful downtown Des Moines area, filled with history and culture, Principal Park where his beloved Cubs had a Triple-A team, the Capitol Building. I lived in Des Moines for four years and the city meant something to me, but apparently eight hours was too long of a trek for him to take with me.

Realizing that my thoughts had completed wandered away from my task at hand—practicing—I tore my earbuds out and tossed them on the bed. Now I felt riled up all over again because I let myself think about Deacon. Why didn't I stand up for myself in that situation? Des Moines was important, seeing Rose and Lalani was important to me. I should have gone by myself, but I really wanted Deacon by my side. We hadn't been together all that long at the time, but it would have been nice to introduce him to my college friends.

Well, maybe not. Because then they would be expecting wedding invitations and not my sob story. Maybe it all worked out for the better.

"Clemmie! Come here, girl! You want to go for a walk?"

Clemmie came bounding into my bedroom, tongue hanging out, telltale crease marks in her fur to show me she had been curled up in her favorite spot on the leather couch, taking a snooze while I worked.

"Come on, girl. Let's see if maybe we can run into Harrison today. You like him, don't you?"

Her tail thumped the ground, which I took as a yes. Even though it was a Wednesday afternoon, I thought I could give it a chance. Talking to him, even though in only short little bursts when we casually ran into each other (now on the same day and times and path on the weekends), lifted my mood. And if I didn't run into him, I needed to get away from my thoughts filled with Deacon and focus on a new man that had me very interested.

NELLIE

I had my first abortion when I was fourteen. For someone who was "sexually active" starting at age ten, I was honestly surprised it wasn't sooner that I got knocked up. Especially because the men having sex with me didn't exactly care about protection.

At fourteen, I was pregnant by one of Mom's "friends" who came around about once a month, when he knew Mom was paid. He leeched off her, ate our food, bought booze and drugs for him and Mom, and then fucked us both. He would come into my room after Mom was already passed out and break my spirit. After, I would lose myself in a book, trying to transport myself into the world of baby-sitters and blonde twins.

I didn't understand why I suddenly couldn't keep any of my food down one day. Breakfast made me vomit, I threw up my lunch in the bathroom next to the cafeteria at school, and I started skipping dinner at home because I was tired of the puking. Mom didn't notice I wasn't eating because she wasn't around enough to notice—or care.

Finally, a girl at school told me I was probably pregnant when she heard me retching in the bathroom for the fourth consecutive day. I had just stared at her, confused. Pregnant? How the fuck . . . why the fuck . . . what the fuck was I supposed to do?

I walked myself to the pharmacy after school that same day, grabbed a test off the shelf, and without bothering to pay for it, walked into the one-stall bathroom and peed on the goddamn stick. A smiley face stared back at me two minutes later. Really? A smiley face? I was fucking fourteen years old and pregnant via rape by a guy my mother willing invited in our trailer. A fucking smiley face?

I didn't cry. I didn't shed a tear for the injustice that was my life. I didn't bother to think why me. Because what the fuck would that have done? Made me un-pregnant?

Instead, I walked out of the CVS, walked myself home, and got out the phone book once I was in the trailer. I called the clinic and scheduled an appointment for the following Friday.

I'd experienced pain in my life, including losing my virginity at the age of ten to a forty-year-old well-endowed man, but nothing compared to that first abortion. It felt like my entire insides had been knifed and then lit on fire. When I came to from the procedure, I cried. I finally broke and cried, not only because of the pain, but because of the goddamn injustice.

The nurse in the room just clucked her tongue, surely thinking I was a promiscuous teen that found myself in a precarious situation. If only I could tell the truth. If only telling the truth would actually do something.

* * *

I had my second abortion when I was seventeen. I was

pregnant by one of the guys I was seeing—or having regular sex with—and when I told him, he roughed me up pretty bad. A lot of the blows were to my stomach, like he was trying to save me the doctor bill or something. I ended up in the ER that night and had an emergency D&C. When the doctors were in there, they noticed some abnormal scarring on one of my fallopian tubes, which was thought to have happened in the first abortion.

The doctor on call that night spoke with me for some time about the scarring and the complications it could have on my body in the future. I didn't care. He also made me speak to a detective. I told him I was jumped in an alley and couldn't really remember what the attacker looked like. No charges were filed, and I wasn't pregnant anymore. I never saw that guy again.

* * *

My third and final abortion occurred just eight months before I met Harrison. I went so many years not getting knocked up that I honestly thought my body just couldn't make a baby anymore, not after everything I had put it through with the sex, drugs, and regular beatings. But I was wrong.

I'm not sure who the father was of that one. It occurred during my hooking days, when I was having sex up to ten times a day with ten different men—sometimes women, though, obviously none of them knocked me up. But it didn't matter who the father was. Once I noticed my tits were hurting and my taste buds seemed to be off—semen had never tasted so sour to me—I took a test, called a Planned Parenthood, and got rid of it.

During that procedure, the doctor said my body had suffered too greatly to ever reproduce. Three abortions must do that. Whatever. I didn't care at the time. I honestly didn't think I was going to even live all that much longer. Who cared that I couldn't have kids? Who knows how the fuck they would turn out anyway? I was following my mom's path at that time, and she ended up dead because of her choices. Why would I ever wish that on some innocent kid?

The doctor suggested I have a full hysterectomy, but I didn't have the money for that shit. Nor did I care. All that mattered to me was that I didn't have to fear getting pregnant anymore, didn't have to have another abortion and waste more money on getting rid of the damn mistakes. I could just move on.

I never expected to meet my husband just months later. Meet a good guy, someone who would fall in love with me . . . just not the real me. Marry into a good family and to someone who wanted to be a dad. Who thought I would make a great mom one day. And who made me want to change my life for the better. Who made me . . . maybe want to be a mom one day. I never thought a situation like this would happen to me. But now it was too late for us to be biological parents. My past had ruined that for us.

If only Harrison knew the real me. But if he did, he never would have married me. I had to keep the real me hidden if I wanted to stay married and in this life.

Chapter 13

NELLIE

Well, my chat with Prue didn't quite go as planned. I was going to tell her the truth about everything, but once I started explaining, I could tell she just wouldn't get it. So I had to make up something on the fly, and hopefully that all made sense. And hopefully I could remember what exactly I told her. In my past life when all I did was lie and exaggerate, I would tend to get my stories mixed up. But I could keep this together. I had to.

But I had figured out the perfect plan, and that was really all that mattered. I would get that hysterectomy that I was told I needed when I was just in my early twenties. I wasn't quite sure yet all the details—I obviously couldn't have a doctor telling my husband and mother-in-law that I needed the surgery due to too many abortions before I was twenty. But would they even know? I didn't have to tell them I had any. It could just be chalked up to . . . genetics or something. Maybe when I saw the doctor I could make up a family history. How would they ever know? Then when they did the examination they would find all these problems, blame my mom and my maternal grandmother and her mother, and I would get the surgery. Problem solved, and it was like . . . halfway truthful.

I worked out vigilantly Thursday morning, forcing myself to double up on Jillian Michaels while I thought through everything. Vernie (Harrison's mother) would be upset, probably more pissed than anything, but if I had legitimate health problems, then what could she do? It wasn't like Harrison would divorce me over something like this. Sure, he would be upset and sad, but he would get over it. Maybe even down the road, like way down the road, we could talk about other options. Adopt a kid and give them a better life, like I always wished had been my story. We could give a child a new story.

When my hour with Jillian was finally up, I collapsed on the floor, feeling like I could vomit or pass out or both. But I felt better. I had a new plan. Harrison just wouldn't understand my past. He could never forgive me for having three abortions and hiding them all from him. He wanted babies. And I felt truly terrible that I couldn't give them to him.

But something else was bothering me. Calvin. I didn't worry that I would start up an affair. I was stronger than that now. I loved Harrison. But how could we all coexist in this small town without the possibility of my past affair coming to light? I had that women's intuition, that gut feeling that trouble was brewing. At some point, my past was going to come back to haunt me, and Harrison wouldn't stay by me. Why would he? I was a horrible person. I had lied to my husband for years. I didn't deserve him to stay with me. And why even entertain the thought of bringing a baby into this? An innocent baby who didn't have a chance at their mother and father staying together. No. It wasn't right. It was just another sign pointing me toward going through with the surgery.

Harrison appeared to be lurking in the kitchen when I came up the stairs. He wasn't reading the paper, he wasn't drinking coffee, he wasn't on his phone. He was just standing there, I think, waiting for me. Damn it. I had hoped he had left already.

"Hey," I panted, wiping the back of my neck with a towel.

"Morning. I would kiss you but." He gestured toward my sweaty face.

I laughed. "I'm not mad. What's up?"

"Do you have plans tonight?"

Now what was he putting us up to?

I shook my head slowly. "Not that I can think of."

"I was wondering if you might like to have dinner with Art and his wife. I haven't made the plans yet, but he's been dropping hints all week that he would like to get together."

Art. A creepy partner at his firm that tried to make a move on me every time we were in a room together. He was disgusting and had the longest, most gnarly fingers I had ever seen. When he would caress my arm, I couldn't help but shudder. When those fingers squeezed my hand as a greeting, I wanted to hurl all over his expensive suits.

"Actually." I tried to give Harrison a coy smile. "I have some news I wanted to share with you. Maybe if you haven't made the plans yet we can skip that dinner and have something here at the house instead?"

He raised his eyebrows. "Oh really? Any hints?"

I shook my head, feeling my hair stick to my damp neck. I needed a shower, and quick. "Nope. Just something that I think you'll be happy with. Now get to work. I need to shower and get ready."

He leaned down to kiss me on the lips, and I obliged.

"I love you."

"I love you, too," I answered. "Have a good day."

"You as well."

While I showered, I thought about how I would tell Harrison that I was going to schedule a doctor's appointment to focus on my fertility. I was going to let the idea sink in for a while yet, trying to make sure all my cards were in place, but I couldn't stand the thought of going out with Art and another boring suburb dinner. I was feeling too anxious. I knew Harrison would tell his mom right away, so I would have to deal with her phone calls and know-it-all conversations and doctor recommendations, but I would get it figured out. After all, I always did.

* * *

Harrison, as expected, nearly lost his mind when I told him the big news over our dinner ordered in from Martin's that night.

"You'll really do the appointment?" he asked, his eyes wide in near disbelief. "What changed your mind?"

"Honestly?" I set down my fork and looked him the

eyes. "I know it means a lot to you. And of course, to your mother. And like you said, what can one appointment hurt? I'll go in, make sure I'm all good, and then it's done and over with."

"So then you want to start trying?" I thought he was going to jump out of his seat in happiness, and I realized my heart really hurt knowing what our future held. I might not have been a good person when I first met Harrison, but I did love my husband now. I did want to make him happy, and this was hard on me, too. I didn't want to imagine the future disappointment when I had to deliver my news.

"I don't know if I'm 100% there yet," I said to him, picking my fork back up. "But I'm getting there. Seriously."

"Wow." He leaned back in the chair. "Thank you, Nellie. I can't say how much I appreciate this. You really . . . I mean, I'm just a little surprised I guess. But happy. Really happy."

Later that night, after we enthusiastically made love and Harrison was in the shower, I rolled over and looked at my cell phone, pulling up the schedule at the salon for the next day.

The first morning appointment made my blood freeze. Calvin. What the fuck?

Chapter 14

PRUE

I had decided to do it. I was going to ask Harrison out. On . . . a date, I guess. There really wasn't a better word for it. I was tired of all the sexual tension, if you will, during our now-obvious scheduled run-ins while I was walking Clemmie and he was running. But, with winter just waiting around the corner, I knew our streets would soon enough be covered in snow and ice and it might get harder and harder for me and Clem to get out there in the crazy weather and freezing temperatures. So I was going to make the first move. I wasn't surprised he didn't make the first move, obviously, and I was ready to stop being meek little Prue. I saw what I wanted, and nothing was going to stop me from going after it. Not anymore.

That Friday, I made sure to put in extra time getting ready for a walk, even though I tried to tell myself it was because I was going to school after and then meeting with Linds for an early dinner. But mostly it was because of this walk.

After giving myself a final look in the mirror, I slipped on my shoes and called to Clem, who came barreling into the room with a stuffed squirrel in her mouth.

"You want to go for a walk, girl? You want to go for a walk, you big silly bear?" I asked her, giving her head a rub.

She promptly dropped the squirrel and spun in a circle, doing a happy dance for her good fortune. I clipped her leash on and off we went, my heart beating fast.

As we approached our usual meeting spot, I slowed down. No Harrison yet. I let myself take a few deep breaths, going over the words I had carefully thought of earlier. When I finally spotted his form coming into view, I let out a breath. Don't show nerves, I reminded myself. It would make this whole thing seem silly if I acted like a darn teenager.

"Well, hi there," he said as he approached, his cheeks already pretty red from the biting wind. He bent down and gave Clem a pat, and her thick tail waved happily.

"Hi. How are you?" I asked, trying to sound normal.

"Cold!"

We both laughed, able to see puffs of breath in front of our faces.

"I understand. Our walks are about to be cut down, aren't they, girl?" I petted Clemmie as well, our hands brushing against each other just briefly on the top of her head. I needed to cut to the chase. I mean, it was cold.

"Aw, poor girl. She must not like the winters much then."

"This will be her first one actually. She'll turn one in the spring."

"Well, you're just a pup then!" he exclaimed. "I didn't realize she was so young. She's so . . . big."

We laughed again. "She was nine pounds already when we picked her up."

"We?"

Shoot. Did I really say we? Harrison and I had never discussed anything personal on our run-ins. I really didn't want to bring up an ex-boyfriend then ask him out. That would sound . . . weird. A tiny white lie wouldn't hurt, right? In the greater scheme of things.

"Oh, me and a friend. Anyway, I actually had a question." I glossed over his question as casually as I could. Did it work? Maybe.

"Yeah?"

"I was just wondering . . . if maybe you might want to grab coffee sometime or something. Because we might not walk much longer, with the weather changing and all. And it makes me a little sad that our chats might end until next spring." Or forever. Who knew where either of us would be next year? I knew my future was certainly up in the air.

He looked thoughtful, and there was an awkward silence. What gave me the idea to do this? Why did I think he would actually say yes to me? Would it be weird if I just turned around and walked away? It wasn't like we actually knew each other or would see each other again. I could just put this whole humiliating experience behind me and—

"Yes."

I looked up to see Harrison smiling. And by up, I mean, up. I realized how much taller he was than me, though that's pretty much everyone. But still. It made him even sexier.

"Really?" I couldn't help asking, then immediately felt like a dummy. Way to give away how nervous and unsure of myself I was.

"Sure. Yeah." He almost sounded unsure of himself, liking he was warming up to the idea. That didn't make me feel great, but he said yes! He said yes!

"Oh. Okay. Great. Then." I tripped over each word, confused. He was saying yes but it didn't look like he really meant it. Was he happy? Doing it to not make me feel embarrassed? I hated this.

"When were you thinking?"

"Oh. Um." I hadn't really gotten that far, honestly, but my mind raced with locations. I recalled the name of his firm, which I knew was on the outskirts of town, near the train station. "Somewhere by your work maybe?"

He nodded, listing off a location I knew I would have to Google when I got home, as the name was unfamiliar to me.

"That sounds good. Thursday?"

"Sure. Nine o'clock maybe?" he asked, looking at me intently. His blue eyes would make me blush, if my cheeks weren't already so red from the cold.

"Perfect. I'm going to get us back inside before I lose a toe to frostbite, but if I don't see you before then, I'll just see you on Thursday."

"Thursday. Nine o'clock. Coffee. See you then." He smiled and I turned around to leave.

As Clemmie and I walked a quick pace back home, I looked over my shoulder to see him still standing there, staring into space. I still wasn't sure he was totally excited about the prospect of seeing me in a more personal setting, but he said yes. Why would he say yes if he didn't really want to? I tried to ignore the little niggle as well as asking why the hell he was saying yes to me, when he had a wife at home.

* * *

"What's gotten in to you today?"

"What do you mean?" I asked my mom, who had walked into the school cafeteria during fifth grade lunch, the last lunch period of the day.

"I've seen you walking around with a goofy smile on your face all day. I even saw you smile while cleaning up that kindergartener who spilled tomato soup all over himself, and I know you hate the smell of tomato soup."

I grimaced a little, remembering little dark-haired Tom in kindergarten (such an old-man name for this tiny little boy) who sat down and promptly tipped his cup of red, smelly soup all over himself. Luckily the soup wasn't hot enough to burn him, but his clothes were ruined. I tried to clean him up as best as I could with a paper towel but ended up walking him down to the lost and found to get him dressed in a dry pair of clothes to see the day out with. After bundling up his clothes in a plastic baggy and labeling them with his name, I went to his classroom to hand them off to the teacher so she could make sure they went home with him. Poor Tom.

"Yeah, that smell is just awful, isn't it?"

"I don't mind tomato soup. But you're avoiding the question."

"Hold on." I zoomed off toward Caleb, who was waving his hand around.

"What do you need?" I asked as I approached.

"Can I have more ketchup?"

I looked at his plate, which had grilled cheese crusts and some celery sticks on it. "What do you need ketchup for?"

"My sandwich."

I looked again. "You don't have a sandwich."

"The crusts! I can't eat them without ketchup."

I sighed but went to grab the ketchup bottle and handed it to him. Usually for the fourth and fifth graders I let them handle dispensing their own ketchup, the littler ones tend to make a mess or go overboard, but I grabbed the bottle out of his hand when it was clear he was just messing around and creating a giant smiley face on his tray.

"Caleb, you know better than that."

"Sorry!" he singsonged as I walked away, shaking my head.

Mom was by my side again in an instant.

"Prue."

"Principal Doherty."

"Are you really not going to tell me?"

"In the lunchroom?"

"Fine. Come to my office after this then."

I sighed. "Fine."

Mom was quite enthusiastic about the news she received after the fifth grade class was dismissed and the lunchroom was back in order. I sat across her desk and told her about the man that I had met on my walks, how nice and friendly he seemed, the connection I thought we had from our brief chats together, and our coffee date lined up for Thursday.

"Well, this certainly sounds like a promising start. What's his name?"

"His name is Harrison and he's a lawyer at Sweeny & Co. And he likes to jog and doesn't mind cold weather. He's a Bears fan and Cubs fan, obviously, and likes sports. And that's really all I know about him, honestly." I didn't look her in the eye.

Mom sat back and tented her fingers. "Well, sounds like you have a lot to find out about him then."

Chapter 15

NELLIE

I stormed into the salon the next morning, and Kerri was already behind the desk.

"Hey, Nellie. Whoa. Are you okay?"

"I'm fine." I smiled tightly. "I'm just going to head into my office, okay?"

She nodded, looking at me warily. "I brought you a Starbies," she said, handing me a tall cup. I took it with a forced smile and tried to calmly walk away, feeling her eyes on me as I retreated to my safe space, and quickly booted up my computer to watch for when Calvin's name became highlighted. Right on time. Bastard.

A knock sounded, causing me to jump. "Hey, Nellie. A customer out here is asking for you."

Fucking bastard.

"I'll be right out."

I looked in the mirror before leaving, making sure I didn't have lipstick on my teeth and that my hair was in place. I threw my shoulders back and walked confidently out to the front lobby, where Calvin was standing, looking comfortable and casual in sweatpants and a hooded sweatshirt.

"Hi, I'm Nellie Hawthorne, owner. How do you do?" I stuck my hand out and placed an emphasis on my married name.

He smirked at me. "Right. Calvin Kass. Your name looked familiar when I was on your website. Thought I would come see if you were an old classmate of mine. But I guess not. I think I'm a bit younger."

I bit back a snarky reply. Calvin was twenty-two, not that much younger than me. Bastard.

"Kerri, would you mind running and grabbing the laundry from the dryer? I forgot to unload it when I was here last."

"Yeah, sure. Okay." Kerri walked away quickly, and I knew she knew something was happening between Calvin and me. Shit.

"Why did you block my number?" Calvin asked, as soon as Kerri was gone.

"Why are you here? Why are you in Oamark Park at all?"

"I got a job here."

"Are you following me?"

I wanted to wipe that freaking smirk off his face. "Nells, seriously, do you think I'm following you? I didn't even know this is where you moved to until I saw your picture and business in a flyer I got in my welcome to the town packet they hand out. Charming little town welcome."

I hoped that was true. "That's great then, but you need to leave me alone. I'm married, Calvin. I blocked your number because I don't need anything from my past coming back to haunt me right now. Just please, leave me alone. Act like you don't know me."

He stepped closer to me, placing a hand on my forearm. "But why would I want to forget about you?" he whispered, his hot breath tickling my inner ear. My knees went a little weak.

At the moment, two things happened. Kerri walked back up front with a laundry basket full of towels at the same moment the front door opened and Prue stepped in.

I yanked myself away from Calvin so fast I nearly tripped over myself, and my face burned. I felt like I was caught red-handed, in front of my employee and new friend. Fuck me.

"Kerri, can you show Mr. Kass to his room please and let him know how to run the bed? Thank you."

I turned toward Prue, who looked startled by what she had walked into. "Prue! I didn't know you were coming by today."

"Oh yeah. I was just in the neighborhood and thought I would swing by and see if you wanted to grab a coffee or anything. But if you're busy . . ."

"No! It's good. I'll just let Kerri know." Thank God. Now I wouldn't have to deal with Calvin once he was done tanning. My hands were shaking. I had to get it together. Get it under control.

When Kerri came back to the counter, I let her know I was going to get coffee with Prue and offered to bring her one back with me. She turned one down and showed me her Starbucks cup, and I had completely forgotten she had picked one up for me this morning. I felt like even more of an idiot. I passed Sasha, another employee, as I walked out the door, and I felt better knowing Kerri wouldn't be alone in case the salon got busy as I took an unscheduled break. Prue and I were quiet as we walked down to the coffee shop, ordered hot drinks, and then sat down.

"How's your morning been?" I tried to lead off the conversation with her talking, to avoid talking about me.

"Um, fine. Nellie? Are you . . . okay?"

"I'm great!" I smiled brightly.

"Did you know that guy? He seemed . . . strange."

"Oh. He's someone I used to know. But it's nothing."

She nodded slowly, but her unwavering gaze sent a tickle up my spine.

* * *

That night, Harrison and I sat down for dinner together, and I tried to talk—really talk—to my husband. I wanted to be a better wife. I wanted to get it together and stop feeling afraid Calvin was going to try to ruin everything for us. But after twenty-nine years of my life, and everything I had done to deceive Harrison, how does one even begin that? How did I get a new beginning, a fresh start? I didn't think Harrison would stay with me if he knew the whole truth and nothing but the truth about his wife, the girl who had duped him into thinking she was someone else so many years ago. The girl that had a plan to slowly rob him of his precious belongings so she could sell them to make money for her drug addiction but ended up falling in love with this kind, good-hearted man. How could he ever forgive me if he knew? How could he ever love me? How could anyone?

My plan to reconnect over deep dish pizza and salad (pizza for him, salad for me) didn't quite go as planned. Harrison seemed lost in thought, distracted, unfocused. I tried talking about his work, about the Bears pulling off a miraculous win, about how disappointed he was that the Cubs lost in the Championship round to knock them out of the playoffs. Nothing seemed to be working, and I was getting frustrated. Why was my husband on another planet?

"I'm sorry, what did you say?" he asked for what felt like the tenth time in ten minutes.

I put my fork down. "Harrison, is everything okay?"

He frowned, looking down at his plate. "Yeah. Is everything okay with you?"

My frown matched his. Why wouldn't it be all okay with me? I wasn't the one acting any different. "Um, yes. You just seem—distracted or something. Is everything going all right at work?"

"Yes."

"Ooookay." I dragged out the word, still watching him. What was his deal?

"Do you still feel the same way about the whole baby thing?" he asked.

So that's what this was about? Was he still worried about it or thinking I wouldn't go through with it?

"Yes. Of course. The soonest appointment I could get in for was in two weeks."

He looked me, his eyes showing surprise. "You booked an appointment."

"I told you I would." I tried not to sound harsh, but come on. Did he think I was a liar or something?

"Wow. Okay. I just didn't know—I thought maybe you might have changed your mind or something—but that's great. Thank you. I know Mom will be thrilled."

I smiled, my lips pressed together. "Yeah. Thrilled."

"Are you happy?" he asked quickly, then almost looked confused that he spoke those words.

I felt an icy shiver along my spine. Why was he asking that? Here, now, tonight? I had an inkling of foreboding, but I didn't know why.

"Of course I am," I said slowly, still leaving my food untouched. "Are you?"

He continued to look at his food, and time seemed to slow down. What had happened here? When did this shift occur? What did I do wrong?

Finally, he looked up at me and nodded. "I am."

But something was wrong. And I didn't know how the hell to fix it.

NELLIE

Four Years Prior

I sat on the toilet, trying to get my thoughts together. Was this rock bottom? Was I officially at the end? How could life possibly go up from here?

"Did you see Harrison Hawthorne at the bar?" A high-pitched voice squealed suddenly, and I heard the clacks of high heels in the bathroom. "Serena was right. He does come on Tuesday nights!"

Both started laughing, and I heard what I figured to be compacts opening and the girls touching up their makeup. I touched my still-bruised eye, covered with pounds of concealer that I had stolen from a Sephora store.

"Are you going to talk to him?"

"Duh. Have you heard how much money his family has? And he's going to be a lawyer just like my dear old dad and his old man. I already fit in! Serena said his parents are starting to pressure him to settle down because it looks better to have an associate who is married than some kid-bachelor. Enter, me!"

"Why not me?"

"Because you're going home with Danny every night."

"Oh yeah. Okay. So how are you going to get together?"

There was silence, and then giggles. I tried to imagine what this girl did. Push up her boobs? Make a blow-job face?

"And just think—if it doesn't work tonight, he's here every Tuesday. You'll reel him in. And buy me a new car once you're married for helping!"

The girls tittered and left, the sound of their heels on the cement floor burning my ears.

My mind was racing. Harrison Hawthorne didn't ring any bells to me, but why would it? I didn't follow things like politics or law or sports. I followed drugs, sex, and money. That's who I was.

I wandered back out to the bar, taking a seat at a small table, alone. Though I didn't wear a sign that said "Will fuck for money" guys just knew. So I waited.

The first guy to approach me was a worker. "Can I get you something? Quarter draws tonight."

I smiled weakly at him. "Just a water, please."

His eyebrows flickered once. "You got it."

When he came back with a tall glass of ice water, I took a drink and tried to calm my scattered mind. I pressed my thumbnails into my palms, probably drawing blood. I wanted a drink, and bad. And something else to dull the pain and make my hands stop shaking. Withdrawals were a bitch. This was what, my fifth time attempting to get clean? I knew it would only get worse from here.

The next week and then the next, I went back to that bar, watching the girls fawn over this Harrison. I stuck with my water, every so often eating greasy nachos or cheeseballs some guy bought me while he sat with me and chatted. Apparently, even when I wasn't trying to put out the whore vibe, I still attracted guys. I tried not to think about what that said about me.

But I didn't go home with them. I went home alone each night, clean and sober. I lay in my bed alone, shaking and vomiting, my body craving drugs.

The fourth week I went back, I was ready. My bruises had finally faded, and though I was still fighting withdrawal effects, I was confident. I could get through one night. I had a half-assed plan, and I wanted to put it to work.

I put a lot of effort into what I looked like that night. I didn't want Harrison to be able to recognize me as the drugged-out girl from previous weeks, sucking down waters and letting douchebag guys talk her up each Tuesday. I needed to put out a different vibe, a different persona.

Earlier that day I had gone to get a free makeover at a store in the mall. I let them load up my face with all kinds of crazy makeup products that no woman should need— and when they told me the prices, that no one should ever spend that kind of money on—and then politely declined buying anything when they were done. Fuck that.

I had a few nice dresses that I stole from a roommate once and put those on, along with the nicest pair of shoes I had. I didn't look half bad.

I tried to think confident thoughts as I walked into the bar, sitting three spots down from where Harrison always sat with a few buddies. I ordered a white wine, to go along with the classy vibe I was putting out, and pulled out a Vogue magazine to flip the pages and gawk at the styles and fashions that were supposedly "in."

Fifteen minutes after I sat down, Harrison came in, taking his usual place. Five minutes later, he was leaning across the empty seats, his hand outstretched.

"Hi, I'm Harrison Hawthorne."

"Nellie Cauler. So nice to meet you."

"Same to you. Do you come here often?"

And the plan was in motion.

Chapter 16

PRUE

Thursday. I arrived at the coffee shop first and was trying not to stare at the door. I caught myself tapping my shoe against the chair leg repeatedly and willed myself to stop. I tried to focus on the newspaper in front of me, but I couldn't make out any of the words. He wasn't coming. Technically, he still had three minutes to get here, but something was telling me he wasn't going to make it. Well, it would be a nice, clean break then. I could stop walking Clemmie on that route, and by next spring, he would be a distant memory. No one would have to know he stood me up—except my mother. Dang it. I knew she would be disappointed too, even though I tried not to talk this up too much.

I was just starting to focus on the article talking about the upcoming presidential election when I heard his voice beside me.

"Prue?"

I nearly jumped out of my skin I was so startled. I did manage to knock my coffee over, effectively spilling the liquid down the table and nearly onto Harrison's shiny black shoes.

"I'm so sorry! I didn't mean to scare you!" he said, taking the sole napkin he was holding and trying to mop up the spill. It did no good.

"No, it's okay! Let me grab some napkins!" I flew to the front counter and grabbed out a wad, rushing back to the table and trying to clear it up. I could tell my face was flaming. I wasn't a clumsy person. So what the hell was I doing? What was wrong with me?

"There. I think that's pretty good."

I smiled at Harrison and went to dispose of the soggy mess of napkins, and to give myself a breather. Stay cool. *It's just a guy. You are not fourteen. Don't act like it.*

I went back to the table where Harrison was still standing.

"Please, have a seat," I said, gesturing to the empty chair like I was about to give a job interview. Smooth.

"Thanks." He took off his coat and gloves, setting them on the back of the chair before sliding in.

I picked up the newspaper, now a bit soggy, then put it back down. I had no idea what to say. Now that the moment of truth was actually here, I didn't know how to act.

"Have you been here before?"

Thank God he asked a question!

"I haven't. I don't usually get out much besides just

around the apartment. I don't like to go too far now with Clemmie at home. She's made me more of a homebody than I ever was."

He smiled. "She seems like a great dog."

I nodded. "She really is. A very loyal companion."

Silence again. Man, this was hard.

"Can I just say—are you feeling as awkward as me? I hope you don't take offense to that?"

"Yes!" I blurted out, then tried to backtrack. "I mean, yes, I feel awkward, not that I was taking offense."

We both laughed, and I could feel myself relax just slightly. While he was looking down, I snuck a look at his ring finger. No wedding ring. Wow. That was interesting.

"Do you have to go to your mom's school today?"

I leaned back in my chair. "Not today. Tomorrow probably. Thursday never seems to be a day that she calls for help."

"I'm so sorry," he said suddenly, causing me to tilt my head. What could he possibly be apologizing for? "Do you want me to get you another coffee? I didn't even ask."

"Oh! Oh, no, that's fine. I already had two cups at home too, so that was probably the higher power's way of telling me that I have enough in my system right now."

He smiled at me, and I couldn't help but admire his teeth—so straight, so white, and surrounded by full lips. They weren't crazy pouty or feminine, but they looked so soft and—kissable. I tried to shake those thoughts away. Focus. There was plenty of time for that.

"Okay, then."

And silence again. Ugh. "What are you drinking?" I finally managed to ask, only about the lamest question out there.

"Just good ole black coffee. Nothing fancy for me."

"I can appreciate that. I try to avoid any Starbucks if I can, but on the off-chance I go in there, I feel like I have to speak a different language to give my order. It's a little on the ridiculous side."

"I agree. So tell me, any big cases coming up that you have to work on?"

I perked up. How had I forgotten this when I was struggling to think of what to talk about? We actually had common ground. "Actually, yes."

I told him all about the upcoming case, where it was taking place and who the firm was that my company was representing. Of course, he was familiar with not only the firm but the case in general, and the next half an hour absolutely flew by and we chatted like two old friends. It was crazy. It was unexpected. But it felt so—right.

After about forty minutes total of us being there, Harrison glanced at his watch and shot me an apologetic look. "I'm really sorry to cut this off, but I do have to get into the office."

"I completely understand. I should probably get home as well. I still have some more research to do."

"You let me know if you have any questions that come up, okay? Either before or during the trial. I'm happy to help out, do what I can."

"Okay, thanks." I waited, but he didn't offer me his phone number, ask for mine, or even hand me his card. Okay . . .

I was just about to ask him myself, when he grabbed his coat and slipped it on, and suddenly I felt too awkward.

I asked him here, why I should I have to ask for his number, too? And he offered his assistance, so clearly . . . the ball was in his court. And I couldn't come off as too needy, too early. That could blow everything.

"What's your first scheduled off-shift?" he asked, slipping his gloves on and pulling a key ring from his coat pocket.

"Not until Friday."

He nodded. "Friday. Do you want to meet again on Friday? You can ask me any questions that might have come up?"

I nodded slowly, a smile forming on my face. "Friday. For questions. Yeah, that sounds good. Sure."

"Here? Same time?"

I nodded again. "Sounds perfect."

"Okay then." He looked like he was ready to leave, but he was just standing there, that same odd look on his face that he had after I initially asked him out. Was he wondering what he was doing? Was he thinking about her?

With a friendly wave, he finally left, and I sat at the table alone, thinking through everything. I was going down a dangerous path, but I didn't care.

Chapter 17

NELLIE

Over the next week, I tried to watch Harrison carefully. I didn't ask him again if he was happy, mostly because I was afraid of what he was going to say. Was he suddenly unhappy? With me? Our marriage? Did he have any idea of Calvin? Of my past?

I was so confused and had no one to turn to. I thought over and over again about going to Prue; after all, she came to me with her relationship issues, but I didn't know if I could trust her. Not that I ever thought we would become BFFs down the line or anything, I'm not into all the shit, but it just didn't feel right going to her. And I had no other close friends, no other family to turn to. The only family I had was Harrison's family, and they never exactly . . . warmed up to me, I would say.

So, I kept quiet, kept my head down, and tried to

make Harrison happy. He wanted sex on Tuesday, Thursday, and Friday nights, I gave it to him. He wanted to have dinner with fucking creepy Art and his wife, I went. He mentioned wanting to see the Bears game, I went out and bought the tickets myself and surprised him with them on Saturday night.

He seemed happy, but still I felt like there was a disconnect, and I didn't know what to do to get everything back to normal. I felt like something larger was at play here, and that it should be obvious. But what? The only thing I could think of was Calvin, but I couldn't just come out and ask Harrison if he knew about my fucking affair. What if Calvin had shown up at his work or something? Or called him?

We enjoyed the game together at Soldier Field, even though I couldn't understand football to save my life and thought the sport in general was borderline ridiculous. It was also freezing, so standing outside for a total of five hours when you included tailgating and then the horrendous walk back to the train did not put me in any better of a mood. But when Harrison questioned me on my sour attitude, I tried my hardest to turn it around.

I did not spend so many years of my life getting to this point to let it all crash and burn now. I did not work my ass off transforming into someone that Harrison Hawthorne could fall in love with, marry, and have a happily ever after with. And I was happy with who I was, who I had turned out to be. Never in my wildest dreams did I think this could happen, but it did. And it felt right. Did I truly think we would be together forever? Honestly? Yes. Because I would do whatever it took to keep him happy. If he suddenly wanted me to turn into a fucking librarian by day and dominatrix by night, I would have. Harrison was the only constant in my life, the only person who loved me––the me he thought he knew anyway. The idea of having to start over with someone new, learning what they liked and who they wanted their partner to be, was exhausting. There was no way I could imagine doing that again, and I didn't want to. I loved my husband. I was good as his wife. Harrison was the partner for me.

I started to actually look forward to this damn doctor's appointment, just so I could have some good news to deliver to Harrison. Well, technically it would end in bad news, but then we could go forth and just live for the next few years while we figured out what to do about the offspring situation. Vernie would get off my back and just let me breathe for a damn minute, even though I was sure her disappointment would probably smother me anytime I was near her.

"Nellie Hawthorne?"

I slipped my cell phone back into my pocket and stood from the waiting room chair, smiling at the bubbly-looking nurse in pink scrubs as she held open the door for me. She had me get on the scale first and I craned my head looking at the numbers with her—116.7. Perfection.

Next we went into a sterile room, where the nurse took my blood pressure and looked over my information sheet that I had filled out after checking in.

"Let's see here—what doctor have you seen before us?"

I pursed my lips. "It's been quite a few years since I've been seen."

She looked up at me, thin blonde eyebrows scrunched up. "Do you know the last time you had a PAP smear?"

I shook my head slowly. "It was probably . . . eight years ago or so."

"Oh. I see." She looked down at my form again. "But you have a family history of ovarian cancer?"

"Yes. My mom and her mom. I'm a little embarrassed to admit that I was always nervous to see a doctor after my mom passed away. I'm afraid of—bad news." I let my voice drop to a whisper at that point, and the nurse looked at me sympathetically, exactly what I was going for with my fake story.

"Mrs. Hawthorne, I understand your concerns. Health is so important, though. I'm just going to ask you a few more questions, okay, and then Dr. Melborne will be in."

"Okay." I clasped my hands in front of me and did my best to put a concentrated look on my face.

"Are you sexually active?"

"Yes. I'm married," I offered.

She clicked a button her tablet. "Monogamous?"

"Excuse me?" What did that bitch just say?

"I'm sorry, it's a standard question. We just need to know how many sexual partners you have."

"Just one. My *husband.*"

"Thank you, Mrs. Hawthorne. How many sexual partners have you had in the past five years?"

"One." Good thing I wasn't hooked up to a lie detector test.

"Are you currently pregnant or trying to get pregnant?"

"Well, no. Not really. I mean, that's a part of why I'm here."

"Sure. We can definitely help answer questions. Are you on birth control? Or using any preventive features right now?"

"Not really. I mean, he doesn't finish . . . you know. In." Why was this so awkward to say? Something about talking to a professional about this stuff made me uncomfortable.

"I understand. Do you self-examine yourself for breast cancer?"

My brow crinkled. "No. Should I?"

"It's recommended all women to do self-exams. It's the first key in detecting anything wrong."

"Oh." Well, my bad.

"Just a few more here." She gave me a sympathetic smile, like she knew this was torturing me. "Do you smoke?"

"No." Ah ha! The truth!

"Drink alcohol?"

"Yes."

"How many drinks a week?"

"A week? Oh, three." Slightly below average, but who counts wine?

"Do you exercise?"

"I do."

"How often would you say?"

"Every day. Usually twice a day." Truth, truth.

I saw her cut her eyes to me and make a note on the sheet. Was she judging me?

"Okay, and do you have a previous doctor we could

get medical records from?"

"I'm not from the area."

She continued to stare at me.

"And I haven't been to a doctor in years, like I said," I clarified.

"Have you gone to a primary doctor? For regular physicals or blood work?"

I shook my head.

"Have you been sick in the past few years? Strep throat, infections? Anything you would need a prescription for?"

"No. I'm a healthy bird." I smiled.

"I see." She looked downright suspicious of me now, and I felt the need to try to make myself look better.

"But I know I need to start seeing a proper doctor. And we want to start trying for a baby and this place came highly recommended by my mother-in-law. Vernie Hawthorne." I hated when I had to name-drop Vernie.

"I understand. Well, I'll just get this to Doctor Melborne and she'll be right in, okay?" The nurse smiled brightly at me, even though I could still sense her unease. Damn it. I should have been more prepared for these inane questions.

"Okay." I tried to match her smile, then let it drop once she closed the door and I put on the paper gown as she instructed, unfolding a rough piece of paper and draping that over my legs. Fuck, I didn't want to do this appointment. It was so invading, so creepy. I remembered PAP smears from years past where the doctors would cheerily chat with you with one hand up inside you, feeling on your organs and probably judging when your last shave was.

I closed my eyes, wondering how soon it would be that I got the results. Would this Dr. Melborne be able to tell just from our first appointment how janked up my insides were? Would she gasp in disbelief and horror, call student doctors in to look at my sad case? Would she be cold and dispassionate, knowing what had been the cause of all this trouble?

I tried again to map out what I would say to Harrison, how to break the news as gently as I could. I had several speeches mentally planned, but nothing felt right yet. Maybe once I had some doctor lingo to throw in there, it would all come together.

NELLIE

Four Years Prior

In my wildest dreams, did I think I could get Harrison Hawthorne to marry me? No. That was not my plan that I devised while listening to a bunch of trust-fund-chasing bimbos talking about him in the bathroom of a downtown Chicago bar.

My plan was much simpler.

Get my way into Harrison's life, then his bed. Get into his home. Slowly but surely steal a few items here and there. Nothing he was bound to notice, at least not right away. Try to get any cash off him that I could. Pawn off my goodies and get enough cash to figure out my next plan in life. I wanted to head out to LA, try my hand at the acting business or something. I probably would have ended up in the adult film scene, so I could see now how thankful I should be that didn't happen.

But my plan didn't go at all as I expected. Did I think Harrison Hawthorne would see me as anything more than a quick lay? That he would somehow find me charming and real and get this—honest? He really used that word.

"You're not like those other girls that try to go out with me," he said the third Tuesday in a row when we were sitting at the bar together. We hadn't ventured outside our Tuesday night "run-ins" yet, but I could tell we were nearly there. I couldn't act too soon; it would blow my cover. I had to have Harrison believe I was just a charming, Midwest girl. Innocent.

I blushed and looked down at my glass of Coke. I

didn't trust myself yet around alcohol, but I didn't want to point that out to Harrison just yet—and why would I be in a bar myself without drinking?—so each week I asked the same bartender to put the coke in a drinking glass versus the big plastic cups they give to non-alcohol drinks and add a garnish with it to make it look alcoholic. Harrison was never the wiser.

"You are. Everyone else hassles me with all these questions about my family and my career, and asking to see my place and do I have a boat." He shakes his head. "I don't know who some of these girls think we are, but we're not the freaking Kennedys. Sure, we're well-off, but man, you would think they think we're royalty or something. A lawyer isn't that big of a deal in a city like Chicago. We're like a dime a dozen."

He was a sweet guy. Sure, his family wasn't the most successful or richest in the city, not even close when you think about all the athletes we have housed in our little town, but Harrison would never have to worry about money. He would never have to dine and dash at a restaurant because he hadn't eaten in three days but didn't have the money to buy anything. He wouldn't have to shoplift clothes when he started to outgrow his but his mom spent all the money on drugs and booze instead of new jeans and shoes. He wouldn't have to sell his body to his landlord when he didn't have the money to cover the rent check month after month. Harrison and I would never be on the same level.

"I'm sorry," he'd said that third week. "I feel like I'm always talking about me and my issues. How can you stand being around someone so negative?" He took a drink of his

Jack and Coke, and then asked, "How about you tell me more about you? All I know is you're from around here, you got stood up by a stupid guy three weeks ago who clearly doesn't realize what he's missing out on, and you're in school at Truman. What do your parents do?"

I had smiled smoothly, prepared for the question. "My life is so uninteresting compared to yours, Harrison." I had leaned in, so my box-dyed dark hair had lightly touched his bare arm, where he had rolled up the sleeves to his dark button-up after his first drink. Just like he had done the past two weeks. One drink, and the sleeves go up. Charming. "But I'm a bit of loner, I'm afraid. My father passed away when I was just a baby, in a house fire. I never knew him, have no memories of him. My mom never remarried to give me any sort of father figure, and she passed away two weeks after I turned eighteen. Cancer."

He'd looked stricken. "Oh, Nellie, I'm so sorry. I had no idea."

I lifted a shoulder. "It's all right. Really. I know it's uncomfortable to talk about so I rarely am the one to bring it up. But I'm okay. I've adjusted to being on my own."

"Do you have any other family?"

I had shaken my head pathetically. "I guess there were some issues between my dad and his family and they didn't even come to his funeral, from what my mom tells me. And I was an only child and so was she. When she was gone, I lost my only family."

I had learned by then how to make myself cry, so I'd wiped away a tear making its way down my left cheek. "Sorry. I really am okay. Just sometimes when I have to think about it, and then when you add it with the drinking . . . my emotions can get the best of me."

"No, no, please don't apologize. Of course." Harrison had placed one of his large hands over my own and gave it a squeeze. "I'm glad you told me, though. I feel like I can really understand you."

I'd given him a small smile. "Thanks. I actually feel a lot better that you know. That you know a part of me, of my past."

And that was the first night I went home with Harrison Hawthorne.

Chapter 18

PRUE

"So, I met a guy."

I was in the office with Linds. I had met her back here after my day in court wrapped. Linds informed me Brandi was out of the office that day, so instead of taking the train back right after court adjourned, I took a cab to the office to play catch-up with Linds.

"What? You did? Tell me more! Tell me everything!"

I laughed. "I will, but quiet down! These cubicles aren't walled, you know."

She looked around sheepishly. "Sorry. I'm just excited. This is the first time you're talking about a guy in . . . you know. Forever."

Forever since Deacon is what she was really saying.

"I know. So, his name is Harrison. He's a lawyer."

"What firm? What's his last name? Is he a partner?

How old is he?" she rattled off, cross-examining me before I could even get another word out.

"Um, whoa. Calm down there, missy."

"I'm sorry!" she squealed again. "I'll try to keep it in check. You may proceed."

"We met on a walk."

"A long walk on the beach?" She looked at me quizzically.

"No." I shook my head. "Just around my apartment and stuff. When I would walk Clemmie, we would run into each other. At first we didn't say anything, then we started to say hi, then he asked me about Clem, and then we kept stopping to chat with each other. He would always be running, but eventually he would stop all together to talk to me and ask questions."

"Wow. I've never really known something like that to happen in real life. It sounds so . . . what am I trying to say? Not like a movie, no. But maybe like a scripted reality show, where the viewers are supposed to think it was totally random these two people met on a walk, but really the show's producers were behind it the whole time. You know?"

I stared at her. "Er . . . yeah. I guess so. Anyway, that's how we met."

She raised her eyebrows. "And then what?! Have you gone on a date? Kissed him? Slept with him? Where are we at here?"

"Sorry, sorry. One of the last times we met on our walk I asked him out for coffee."

"Wait a minute." She put a hand in the air. "You asked him? You asked a guy out on a date?"

"Please don't say that so loud. I don't want anyone to overhear and think I'm suddenly some desperate woman."

"No one would think that. Besides Brandi probably. But okay. But . . . really? I'm just surprised, is all."

"I think I was surprised I went through with it. I was feeling down on myself and looking through the box of me and Deacon." She nodded knowingly, and I knew I wasn't the only one who had an ex-boyfriend box stashed away. "And it just seemed like a good idea. And he said yes. I think I surprised him too, but he agreed to it."

"Have you already gone out with him?"

"We met for coffee last week at a place near his work."

"In Chicago?"

"In Oamark Park."

"Well, I'll be." She leaned back in her chair, looking at me thoughtfully. "And are you meeting again?"

"Tomorrow."

"Prue! That's so amazing. Wow. A lawyer and court reporter, sitting in a tree. Or a courtroom."

"Ha ha."

"Well, tell me more. Do you like him?"

"What kind of question is that, you goof? Of course I like him. But I'm just getting to know him. We haven't really delved into any kind of personal stuff yet. Just safe topics—work and my dog, that sort of thing."

"I get it, I get it. I respect that." She pursed her lips. "Will you tell him about Deacon?"

I tried to tame down my frustration at the question. Why was that always the first thing people questioned? Deacon this and Deacon that. Did I want to come into the office today, Deacon was there? Did I want to go the party for Cherry's birthday? Deacon would be there. When could I just be Prue again and not Deacon's ex that he screwed over?

"I mean, maybe. Probably. If this goes anywhere. I don't think that's really first date conversation. And I don't think we've even been on a real date yet. Grabbing a coffee for thirty minutes before he goes to work is hardly much to write home about."

"But have you told your mom about him?"

"What does that have to do with anything?"

"So you have told Jean!"

"Well, yes. I went to school shortly after our coffee date—meeting—and she could tell something was up with me. So I told her. It wasn't a big deal."

She rolled her eyes. "Now your mom is interested; I'm interested. Hell, it even sounds like your dog is interested."

"Clemmie does seem to like him." I smiled fondly, thinking of how her tail would jump up and down when she saw him.

"This is awesome, Prue. Really. I'm excited for you. I hope tomorrow goes well."

"Me too. I'm hoping maybe he'll ask me out on a real date, too. I don't really want to ask him after asking him out initially. You know? I'm not that forward of a girl."

"Understandable. Well, I'll be thinking good vibes for you. Will you tell me how it goes?"

"Of course." I smiled, happy that she was excited for me. It always helped to have a friend excited and supportive for a life change. Or potential life change.

At home that night, as I was lying in bed, I turned over everything I knew in my mind, Clemmie snoring softly next to me. I rolled over, tucking my body around her large form, feeling the warmth seep over me.

I always prided myself on making the right decisions, the right choices, doing the right thing, and being the good girl. Especially after my dad died, I got weird with karma and thinking that every I dotted and T crossed had to be done just right, or Heaven forbid something else terrible would be bestowed upon me.

But as I was getting older, I wasn't sure I really believed that anymore. I knew deep down I was a good person. I was a good daughter, a good friend, a good worker. I had been a good girlfriend to Deacon, and I didn't deserve the way he treated me, yet it still happened. If I wanted to sit here and continue to play the karma game, I could drive myself insane. At some point, I had to realize that I needed to do what was best for me, every single day. I had to start being a little selfish or else I was always going to get run into the ground by the Deacons and Brandis all over the world. And I didn't want that. I wanted happiness.

But at what cost?

Chapter 19

NELLIE

I met with Prue Friday for a late lunch, and I was a little on edge. My period was coming, so that was the biggest issue, but I was feeling . . . pissed. Harrison was still acting off, I didn't have the results back yet from the doctor, so I couldn't even have the big talk with him so he would be sad and sympathetic toward me and start acting like my caring husband again, and I was still paranoid about Calvin. When would things go back to normal?

Prue said she would meet me directly at the Mediterranean eatery since she was coming from her job. I tried to remember to ask her what her job was during lunch, but at that moment, I truthfully just didn't care. I felt fat, bloated, I could feel a breakout coming on my chin, and I was just pissed off at life.

I ordered the skewers and baklava from Eric, then

took a seat at the table and pulled out my cell phone. The Sephora app was up, and I was frantically adding items to my virtual shopping cart. I wanted to physically go shopping, but with my schedule at the salon today there was no time to get down to Chicago to release my tensions with a shopping spree, so a virtual release would have to do.

Just as I was putting The Big Book of Sexy into my cart (a skincare set costing $389), I saw Prue walk through the door, a smile on her face and her blonde hair in a bouncy ponytail. She looked young, fresh-faced. I seethed with jealousy. I took a breath and tried to rein it in. I should have just canceled this damn lunch.

I watched her closely, chatting with Eric easily now like they were old friends. She said something that made him tip his head back and laugh. Did I make Eric laugh? She paid and then turned and waved to me, walking over. I noticed she wasn't carrying a purse, just a small wallet. We were so different.

"Hi!" she said, taking the seat across from me.

I pushed my lips into a smile. "Hi. How are you today?"

"I'm great." She did this weird sigh thing as she rolled her shoulders back, like she was releasing tension or something.

"Did you do yoga today?" I asked, still looking at her.

She looked confused. "Yoga? Um, no. Why?"

"You remind me of myself after I do a good yoga class. I feel . . . good. Centered. Happy."

She blushed a little. "Oh. Well, no yoga today. Or any day. I don't really work out much. Besides walking with my dog."

I cocked my head in confusion. She wasn't super skinny by any means, but she wasn't fat. Or even chubby. How did she remain that way without a proper workout schedule?

I shook my head. "I wish we could switch lives."

She looked at me oddly. "Why do you say that?"

"You don't work out and you look like that? I'm jealous. If I stopped working out, I would probably blow up like a balloon."

"You're crazy. But you also eat well. I'm always wishing I could eat better. I could live off sugary cereal and potato chips if I had to."

"I haven't had potato chips in years." I sighed, trying to remember what one even tasted like. Not a clue.

"When did you get so into health and fitness?" she asked, looking curious.

I shrugged, but I knew exactly when and why. These are the types of women Harrison's friends dated back when we were still new and who I was trying to emulate. If they went on crazy diets and spent two hours at the gym, then so did I. It helped when some of them realized I wasn't going anywhere and we could buddy up, helping each other learn about new diets, pills, or workouts and personal trainers to hire—or have our men hire for us. When you lived your life a certain way for so long and got so adapted to it, it was hard to change. And I knew it helped me look good. Vanity was real when you started approaching thirty.

"I don't know. It's just been my lifestyle for so long, I guess." That was partly the truth, after all.

She nodded. "I know I'm lucky. My mom is super thin

so I know I have good genes. But even at her age, she's so active. I'm glad I got my dog, because she at least motivates me for walks and stuff."

I just nodded. I couldn't shake this mood for anything.

"Are you close to your mom?" Prue caught me off guard with that question.

"My mom? No, I don't have one." Prue looked startled, so I rushed on. "I mean, anymore. She's passed away. Fire. A house fire. She didn't get out in time."

"Oh my God." Prue looked horrified. "I'm so sorry. I feel so inconsiderate. I didn't realize––"

"You had no way of knowing," I cut her off, trying to smile. "Really. It was a long time ago. It's okay."

Eric came and dropped off our food, then went back to the counter with his signature smile in place. Prue was quiet as she placed a napkin in her lap.

"I promise you I'm not upset," I said, still feeling her unease.

"Okay."

"Can we change the subject yet?" I asked with a smile, relieved when she lifted her head and smiled back at me with a nod.

"Busy day at the salon?" she asked, picking up her gyro.

I exhaled, glad to move on from that conversation. "Oh, yes. Fridays are the busiest for spray tans, that's for sure."

She chewed and nodded, then swallowed and said, "Yeah, I can see that. I want to try a spray tan sometime. Does a machine do it or a real person?"

"We have both options." I slid a vegetable off the skewer, popping it in my mouth and chewing slowly. I just couldn't get my appetite back suddenly. I came in here ravenous, now I could barely eat.

"Do you recommend one or the other?"

"I definitely recommend having one of our girls do it. The machines are pretty much there at getting it applied evenly, but having someone focus on you really makes a difference. And they understand things like shading and contouring and can even spray paint abs on you if you want!"

"Seriously?" Prue's eyes widened. "That's amazing."

"It really is. If you ever want an appointment just let me know. I'll book you with Kara. She's the best we have."

"Okay. I will."

We were quiet again, as she enthusiastically ate her food and I picked at mine, realizing I told Prue how my dad died, not my mom. Well, not my real dad of course because who the hell knew his identity, but the story I told about my father's death. What was wrong with me today? I'd been telling people my mother died of cancer for years. I just couldn't be trusted today. Next thing I knew I would blurt out the real reason she died. Prue would probably faint.

"How was your day?" I asked, remembering my polite manners—and that people loved to talk about themselves.

She put down her sandwich. "It was pretty good actually. I think—well, yeah. I met a guy."

I raised my brows. "Really? Well, that's amazing then."

"Yeah. I mean, it's really new, we haven't really even

been on a proper date, but who knows? It could turn into something."

"I'm sure it could. Is he from work?"

She shook her head. "No, I learned my lesson there. He's from around here. But speaking of work, I had a run-in with Brandi last time I was in."

I struggled with the abrupt switch in conversation. I would think she would be more excited to talk about her new guy, but whatever. Back to the villain. "Oh yeah? How did that go?"

Prue continued to talk while I continued to push around my food. The only item that interested me was the baklava.

"Oh! I almost forgot to ask," she said as we were finishing up our meals. "Did you go to your doctor's appointment?"

"I did. No news yet, but I hope to get the call next week to know what's going on. Fingers crossed for good news and we can start trying for a baby in the near future."

She leveled me with an odd, steely gaze. "Sure. My fingers are crossed."

Chapter 20

PRUE

"Thanks," Nellie said, after I said my fingers were crossed. "I know my husband will be overjoyed if everything is fine. And me, too," she tacked on, looking down at her plate, where she had clearly been pushing her food around instead of eating it. I didn't think she took more than three bites of her skewers.

"Is everything okay?" I asked, looking closely at her. My heart was still pounding loudly after hearing that baby bombshell.

She let out a little sigh. "Oh yeah. I just . . . well, I feel a little silly saying it out loud. Especially to you."

I crinkled my brow. "Me? Why?"

"Well, just with what you've been through. I just. . . I think maybe my husband is in, like, in a funk. I don't feel like we're connecting as well as we usually do."

195

I nodded slowly, digesting her words. I chose my next words carefully. "Any idea why?"

She shook her head, her lips twisted up in confusion. "No. Not really. I keep thinking maybe it's the baby thing, but we don't even have anything to go off yet. Hopefully once the good news results are in he'll go back to normal."

I nodded again, eyeing her closely. "Well, if that's all . . . then it must be nothing to worry about."

She looked at me again, seeming to force a smile. "I'm sure that's it. Just a lot of high tension right now. And I know his mom puts a lot of pressure on him—on us—for babies. So I'm sure that doesn't help."

"He's close with his mom?" I asked before I could stop myself.

She nodded. "Yeah. Sometimes too close, in my opinion."

I shelved that away for later, saying nothing more on the topic.

"But sorry. With everything you have to deal with—especially after hearing about Brandi bitching at you the other day in your professional setting—it just seems a bit trite to say my husband's mood seems off. You know?"

I nodded. "It's okay, though. I think I'm finally starting to move on from that. I actually got a little upset the other day when I was talking to my friend Linds about this guy I met. One of her first questions was if I was going to tell him about Deacon. I mean, yeah, maybe if we go on a real date or something, but we've gotten coffee twice and pretty much only talked about work. He did ask me to lunch next week, so I guess that's something, but I'm not going to start unloading all this crazy baggage before I even know his birthday, you know? And I guess I'm just tired of only being associated with all that crap. I have to move on at some point, right? Why not now?" My heart was beating abnormally fast. I couldn't believe I was saying this to her. Was I a monster?

"Why not now?" Nellie repeated. "That's a really good point, Prue. I'm happy for you. Even just a few weeks ago you seemed like a different person, and now you seem . . . just better. That's really cool."

I felt my face heat up, and it was impossible not to feel guilty. Damn conscious. "Thanks. I'm just happy I finally reached that point, you know? I guess I got worried for a hot minute that I would always be . . . stuck. And I don't want to be stuck."

She nodded again, this time slowly, seeming to look just over my left shoulder and not really at me. "No one deserves to be stuck. No one."

* * *

After I got home from lunch, I played with Clemmie in our small living room, trying to help her get some energy out. It was below twenty degrees outside and a light snow was falling, even though it was still two weeks away from Thanksgiving. I couldn't muster up the enthusiasm to dress warmly enough, so Clem and I played tug of war with one of her rope toys for a while instead.

I was having dinner with my mom that night, so after working on my pages for a few hours, I showered and got dressed just before five, then pulled on dark jeans and a simple black long-sleeved top. I made sure to blow dry my hair so it wouldn't freeze when I went outside, then threw the fluffy strands up in a bun after immediately becoming annoyed at how soft my hair was. Girl problems.

After layering on my coat, scarf, and gloves, Clemmie and I were out the door and in my car, en route to my mom's house, just a quick five-minute drive away. She had steak, mashed potatoes, green bean casserole and homemade rolls waiting, and my stomach immediately started growling when we walked through the door and the smell wafted over to me.

After the greetings were made and while Clem was still sniffing every corner, just to be sure she was properly acclimated to the house she was in at least once a week, Mom said, "Dinner should be ready in just a few minutes. What do you want to drink?"

I waved a hand. "I'll get it, Mom. Why don't you sit down?"

"Oh no. You treat me like I'm an old woman or something." Mom shook her head.

"You managed to survive a Friday without me?" I asked. I told Mom I couldn't be on call while this case was going on because I was basically on call all day every day and couldn't risk not being able to get into the office or the courtroom for anything.

"Oh, we did. The guidance counselor and language arts teachers split the duties today, but I have some good news."

"What's that?" I opened the fridge and took out a can of Coke.

"We have officially hired someone for the position. We just need her background check to clear and then some training, but that's not too difficult for the position. You're almost off the hook!"

I smiled and cracked open the tab. "Aw, that's good, but I'm going to actually miss those kids. And their stories." They started to grow on you after a while.

"And I'm sure they'll miss you. But we can always use you when someone calls in sick or is on vacation, so you'll have opportunities to come back," she said with a smile.

"Good to know."

"All right, I'm famished. Let's eat!"

I helped Mom get the dishes out and we served ourselves, taking our plates to the dining room and sitting across from one another. Clemmie curled up beneath my feet, just waiting for a piece of food to "accidentally" drop from my hands and into her waiting mouth.

"So?" Mom asked, looking at me pointedly from across the table.

"So?" I questioned back, feeling the smirk on my mouth.

"Don't try to play coy, dear, it isn't becoming on anyone. Did you set up a third date?"

I cut into my steak while nodding my head. "Yep. And he asked me!"

"Wonderful! I had a good feeling about this. Tell me more."

"Well, we spent most of the time talking work stuff. We really have a lot in common there."

"Which is excellent." Mom nodded.

"And then just when I thought we were going to go our separate ways, he asked if I wanted to get lunch on Tuesday."

"Where to?"

"Just the café near his work. It sounds like he doesn't get a very long lunch break, so it will probably be just a short one, but I guess that's better than nothing."

Mom eyed me carefully. "Were you perhaps hoping for more of a dinner route?"

I gave a little shrug. "Maybe. On one hand, I feel like we're moving at a snail's pace. All those chats while out walking. Two coffee dates. Now just lunch? On the other hand, why move fast? I don't want to get burned again, that's for sure. Maybe it's better that we go slow."

Mom took a bite of steak and seemed to choose her words carefully. "There are pros and cons to each, you know that. It sounds like you still need to get to know this man. Why rush if perhaps you aren't compatible in the long run?"

"You're right." I was silent for a minute, swirling a piece of steak in ketchup for longer than needed. Why was I frustrated Harrison was moving slow? If he moved quickly, what would that really say about his character? What did any of this say about mine?

"Everything all right, dear?"

"Yeah. It's just . . . I wonder if I'll ever find happiness again. I really worry about it. And what if I don't deserve it?"

"Where is this coming from? Why would you think such thoughts?"

"I don't know, Mom. I'm feeling so conflicted. Like . . . this thing with Deacon. What if it happened for a reason? What if it was like karma in reverse? What if the universe or whoever knew I would make a mistake in the future, and that was my punishment?"

"Prudence Camilla Doherty. Is there something else going on here? I'm shocked you are saying this."

I felt the tears start to threaten and pushed them down. "I don't know. I don't know, Mom. No, nothing else is going on. I'm just . . . hurting. Brandi and I got into it at work the other day and I feel uncomfortable about a lot of things again."

Mom's look went from stricken to soft. "Oh, honey. I'm sorry that happened. She's a dolt. Don't let her get to you. Don't let her—or Deacon, or anyone—make you second guess yourself. Honey, I know how great of a woman I raised. You've made me so proud, year after year. You handle yourself well. You're kind to others. You have one of the biggest hearts of anyone I know. You try your best in every situation you are dealt. And you're usually so positive. It tears me apart to see how this whole ordeal has gotten to you. Rise above it, Prue. Remember what makes you that good person and forget anything else. You deserve to find your happiness. If anyone deserves it, it's you. And I know you'll find it. And when you do, hold on to it, dear. You never know what life will throw at you. I think we both know that."

I absorbed her words. I knew she was talking about my father's death at the end, but a few of her words were ringing in my ears. *"You deserve to find your happiness. If anyone deserves it, it's you."*

I did deserve happiness. I worked for twenty-seven years to be the best person I could be. When did I get a break? When did I get a pardon? Now. I knew it. Now was the time. I felt relief sweep through my body. I deserved this.

"Did you tell me his name?" Mom asked suddenly, looking at me from across the table.

I picked up my fork, grabbing the piece of steak between my teeth and noshing eagerly again.

"Harrison. Harrison Hawthorne."

NELLIE

Four Years Prior

It didn't take me long to completely reel Harrison in. I knew what he wanted. He wanted a good girl, an innocent girl, someone who loved him for him, not for his career or his money. I slowly transformed myself into his dream girl. It was easy. All I had to do was listen. And watch. And process. Then proceed.

When he mentioned how close he was to his family, I insisted we have a family dinner with his parents and was on my best, most becoming behavior the night I met his mom and dad. I dressed right—turtleneck dress that wasn't too tight, heels that we're too high, had my hair professionally styled and my makeup applied at a makeup counter. I brought flowers and a bottle of expensive wine with me that Harrison had picked out (and paid for) but it was in my arms and I brandished my welcoming gift at Mrs. Hawthorne and she delighted in the brand. I rarely talked about myself, instead asking question after question to his family, because really, people only want to talk about themselves. When asked about my family, I smoothly deflected the questions, saying both my parents had sadly passed away, then would talk about how caring and considerate their son was, causing Harrison's father to nod and his mother to beam.

When Harrison would ask me to work events I would stalk the outside of his law firm, watching the characters who came and went. I saw what the women wore, how they styled their hair, the shoes they wore. I made myself out to be the perfect arm candy for one of the hottest young attorneys in Chicago. I was sophisticated and stylish, two words that had never before in my life described me.

Over the first year together, I worked hard on getting my persona down just right. I cut out the swear words. I wore more black and camel and gray, low-slung heels and updos. I learned how to eat right, how to order off menus in French with no prices, how to hold my silverware. I learned small things—how not to fill a wine glass completely to the top when hosting parties, how to fill an appetizer plate with finger food, how to decorate an apartment tastefully. I learned that I enjoyed this new life, this new role I was playing. I liked the stability that came with Harrison.

I secured a job at the Sephora inside the Water Tower and loved my job fiercely. I was surrounded by the products that I once stole as a teenager. I was the one performing makeovers on the girls like I had gotten done the night I wanted to meet Harrison. I was able to buy fancy makeup products and yummy-smelling expensive soaps and silly tools like an eyelash curler with my employee discount and steady paycheck.

And slowly, over time, I did fall in love with Harrison. But by the time I realized I had actually fallen for this man, it was too late to be honest. I had let my lies go too far. I had made him believe too much was different about me. He had fallen in love with a different person than who I really was, and I could never show that side to him, or else I would lose him.

So even though I loved him with all my heart, I didn't know how to be honest with him. But would I take back what I had done? No. Because if I hadn't, Harrison Hawthorne would have never let the real Nellie Cauler get past one conversation with him. I did what had to be done, and I couldn't have regrets about it.

Chapter 21

NELLIE

"I'm sorry, what?"

"Good news, Mrs. Hawthorne! All your tests looked great. I know you had some concerns about fertility, but everything looked just fine. Be sure to give us a call if you get a positive pregnancy test, and we can get you all set up with an OB-GYN."

I was in shock. True, heart-stopping shock. How . . . how could this be? I was told years ago I needed a hysterectomy. That my insides, that my reproductive organs, were basically no good. How could I now be told that I was in great shape to get pregnant? They had to be wrong.

"Mrs. Hawthorne? Are you there?"

I cleared my throat, trying to compose myself. "Um,

yes. Yes, I'm here. I'm sorry, just overwhelmed, I guess."

The nurse on the other end laughed. "Don't worry, honey. I understand."

But did she?

"Do you have any other questions?"

"Ummm . . . no. I guess, not right now." What could I ask? Are you sure? Did you double-check my fallopian tubes? Have you already told my mother-in-law I was in perfect reproduction shape? Oh my God. What was going on? I was totally, fucking confused.

We hung up moments later, and I stumbled into the bathroom, my thoughts racing. I didn't understand how this was possible. Was it possible that I was somehow fixed? That over the years I healed? Did my doctor lie to me when I was a teenager? Did either that doctor or this new doctor miss something? Did Vernie somehow get the doctor to say I was fine? But that wouldn't make sense. But . . . none of this made sense.

"Hey." Harrison suddenly appeared in the doorway, and I yelped and fell back on the bed, my cell phone flying out of my hands and onto the wood floor.

"I'm sorry. I figured you heard me come in. You okay?" Harrison walked a little closer to me, and I reached down to get my phone.

"Yeah, sorry. Just startled."

An awkward silence hung in the air. I didn't really know how to act around Harrison since he had been so strange lately, and now with this news . . . I really didn't know what to do.

"Was someone on the phone?" Did he have suspicion in his voice when he asked me that? Oh God! He did think I was having an affair! Maybe that was why he was so odd. Shit. Shit!

"What? Oh. Well. Actually. It was the doctor's office."

His eyes changed. Relieved. Curious. "Oh yeah? What did they have to say?"

"I . . . they said that I look great. Healthy. That we can start trying for that baby anytime and I should be in good shape."

Harrison's whole face changed.

"Are you serious?"

I nodded, trying to smile. His expression . . . he was so happy.

"That's incredible news, Nell. Wow! Oh my God. That's . . . that's incredible."

He threw his arms around me and next thing I knew, I was being lifted in the air. I put my arms around his neck, laughing a little. Wow. I thought he would be happy—I knew he would be happy—but I wasn't quite expecting this.

He brought me down gently and placed a palm on either side of my cheek, kissing me deeply.

I broke the kiss. "Hey, now. Just because I'm cleared doesn't mean we start trying right now. And we don't even know if you're all healthy and on the up and up."

"Oh, my mom made me do a test weeks ago. I did it to appease her. It came back fine. I didn't want to say anything because I didn't want it to seem like I was pressuring you to do an appointment. But I plan on trying to seduce you tonight, Mrs. Hawthorne. This is terrific news. Thank you so much for doing that. It's a lot of pressure off my mind, and I know my mom will be thrilled."

Ah yes. Vernie would be just thrilled and then firmly up my ass about having a baby. Can't wait.

"I'm happy too, Harrison. But I still would like to wait a little longer before we start trying. I'm not ready for that huge change yet."

He nodded his head, still looking enthused. "That's okay. I just really appreciate you taking the time to do the appointment. I hope you know how much it means to me."

"You're welcome." I leaned in for another kiss, feeling a strange mix of emotions. Feeling conflicted. I still didn't understand the results of my doctor appointment. But now I was in too deep.

* * *

"Ah, well isn't that just delightful news, then." Harrison's mother gazed at me from across the dinner table. Harrison wanted to share the news with her in person, so on the day of my appointment results, he called his mother and said he had exciting news to share and wondered if we could all have dinner together.

His mother's enthusiasm at us having "big news" to share—scheduling five days out. This woman. What if the news was that I was pregnant? For someone who preached class and decorum, she sure lacked it.

I tried to smile at her over the ridiculous centerpiece on the table. I swear, the flower arrangement was at least three feet high, with intensely fragmented flowers spilling out of the gaudy gold vase. Her table was always decorated like we were eating at a wedding—a very gaudy wedding. "Thank you. I was quite sure everything was going to be fine, but I'm happy to put your mind at ease as well," I said, trying not to sound condescending. Harrison hated when I was rude to his mother, but it was pretty damn hard not to be.

"Oh, please, don't make it sound like you did the appointment just for me." She picked up her wine glass and took a delicate sip. "I know how badly my boy wants children, so it was merely a suggestion."

My ass! I took a gulp of wine myself, setting the glass back down with probably more force than necessary. This woman was a bitch. "Yes, well, that's over now."

Her thin eyebrows flickered slightly. "And when will you start trying, now that that's over now?"

Was she mocking me?

Harrison chimed in. "Not right away, but very soon, Mother. You'll be the first to know."

The first to know we were pregnant, or the first to know we were trying? Why did we have to tell anyone we were trying? That was just plain weird. And if she wanted to be the first to know we were pregnant, she would have to schedule us in a little sooner than her normal 5-7 days. For her only son!

"I'll be on the edge of my seat." She shot me another

look, and I tried not to squirm. It was obvious she never liked me, never approved of me, and knew I was hiding something. How she allowed her son to marry me was always a mystery to me. I would have figured she could have dug up something about me or possibly even planted shit like men's underwear or something in our house to try to cause problems. Really. I wouldn't put anything past this woman.

The rest of dinner was a fairly silent affair, with Harrison and his father chatting about the Bears and the North division, and Vernie and I sitting in silence, both pushing around our food and drinking our wine.

Chapter 22

PRUE

Tuesday. It was the day of my lunch date with Harrison, and I was so excited. It was my scheduled day off from the courtroom, and I needed it. Eight hours hunched over my steno machine in the courtroom, followed by at least another four hunched over it at my house or in the office, five days straight, had me exhausted and achy. The worst part—there was no clear-cut end date in sight. The court reporters on this case were getting weary, and tempers were flaring in the office even worse than usual. Brandi was in peak shape, and I was trying my hardest to just stay away from her. Every time we had to be close to one another, her comments about cracked me.

"I'm just starting to decorate *our house* for Christmas. I can't wait to help Deacon hang the lights. The whole block is going to be so cute!"

"Deacon took me on the best surprise date last night! He knows how stressed I've been at work, so he had a whole event planned for us, including a massage to end the night. Well, not end it end it, if you know what I mean."

"I'm just so happy with my life. I have it all right now, you know? How could things possibly get any better?"

She made sure to say it loudly enough that there was no way I would miss what she was saying, and the smug looks she threw my way cut me to the core. I couldn't believe someone could really act that way. She was proud of what she did. There's a difference between going after what you want and feeling no guilt or remorse about who you flatten in your wake. Right?

It was the first day in so many that I didn't have to dress up in a fancy pants suit and heels, so I wanted to go casual. As I was reaching for my basic jeans, I paused. Should I put more effort into my outfit? I looked longingly at my jeans. Nope, jeans it was. I wanted to wear jeans, I would wear jeans. I was feeling more assertive already, after my zillion pep talks to myself and chatting with Mom. I would do what I wanted to do, and that's how it would be. I knew I would be happier because of it. And I really didn't want to even look at my suits or nice dress pants today.

After dressing in jeans, a long-sleeved purple top and a long cardigan, I did minimal makeup and put my hair in a braid. After letting Clemmie outside and then in her kennel with a treat, I put my coat, hat, gloves, and boots on, and headed out to my car.

Another thing I really missed about having my house was the luxury of a garage. There were garages for rent at this complex, but they were already all rented by the time I moved in, and I honestly didn't know if I could afford an extra $400 a month just for a garage. That seemed a little steep, but as my teeth clattered in the frigid air of the car, I started to rethink that steep comment. I couldn't imagine when the snow would start coming and I would have to dig my way out each day that I needed to leave. That reminded me—I needed to find my ice scraper. I was sure it was still in one of my moving boxes, but I would probably need it in the next few weeks.

I drove the short distance to Finns, getting a close parking spot and quickly walking inside. Once in, the heat immediately made me breathe easier. It was toasty in here.

I saw Harrison already sitting at a table, so I walked over to him while unzipping my coat, slinging it onto the back of a chair as I pulled it out.

"Prue. Hi," he said, starting to stand. He was such a gentleman. I couldn't get over his impeccable manners. His mother sure raised him right. I imagined her as a warm woman, someone who loved her son and wanted him to grow up and respect women.

"Hi! Cold one today, huh?" I asked, taking a seat.

He sat back down. "Snow in the forecast next week."

"While it seems soon, I'm excited. I've been waiting to go snowboarding."

His dark eyebrows raised. "You snowboard?"

"Oh yes, I love it! We used to take family trips out to Colorado every year. My dad loved being on the slopes."

"Do you still go?"

"No. My dad died three years ago. My mom and I haven't been back since."

"I'm so sorry."

"It's okay. You didn't know. I don't mention it much. But we always had a lot of fun. Mom wasn't much into the snow, so she usually stayed in the cabin while Dad and I went out, but we always had fun at night up there—dances and taste testings and tours."

"Sounds like a nice time."

"Definitely."

The waitress came by then and set down his drink, then asked for my drink order. After I asked for a Coke and she walked away, Harrison picked up his drink and that's when I noticed a silver band on his left ring finger. This was the first time in all of our time together that I had seen him wear the jewelry that clearly stated he was married. I couldn't tear my eyes away from his wedding ring, and he noticed me looking.

He cleared his throat. "I'm sorry. Part of the reason I asked you to lunch was because I think there might be some confusion. But I am married. Happily married," he added, looking down into his cup. "I'm afraid I've given you the wrong impression, perhaps."

My mind was racing. "Oh. I see. I'm sorry. I guess I never noticed your ring before. And I didn't even think to ask, for some reason. Of course you're married."

"I don't wear my ring when I jog or work out. And sometimes I forget to put it back on before leaving the house, which is why I didn't have it on the two other times. I didn't even think anything of it. Again, I'm really sorry if you had . . . something else in mind. It was careless of me."

My heart was burning. Why was he just now admitting he was married? What had changed? "No, no, it's perfectly fine. I mean, maybe I might have thought there was a spark or something, but to be honest, I'm not in a position to be in a relationship right now. I just enjoyed being able to talk to someone away from the office, but who still understood my job. Like how you understand it. Because you're a lawyer and everything." I realized I was babbling and gratefully smiled as the waitress came back and set down my soda. We gave our order and she walked away, and I took a deep breath before resuming. "I just got out of a pretty bad relationship, and we worked together. And his new girlfriend is also a co-worker. So I moved here to be closer to my mom but haven't really ventured out much yet. You were one of the first friends I made around here."

He grimaced. "I'm sorry to hear that part. That must be tough."

I nodded, not saying anything further. He continued.

"I'm glad we're on the same page, though. I realized I could be acting out of character for someone who is married and just wanted to assure you that I'm not that kind of a guy. I'm always the good guy."

The way he said it made me perk up. "I'm always the good girl. Still, sometimes we finish last, huh?"

He gave a little laugh. "Sometimes. Sometimes."

"When everything happened with my ex, all I could think was why me? Where did I do karma wrong? It's something I've actually been struggling with a little bit lately." This lunch was sure not going as planned, but plans changed. And I intended to roll with it.

He let out a little sigh. "Sometimes I think the same thing. But I really don't have much to complain about, honestly. I have a really good life. Grew up comfortably.

Mom and Dad. Found my wife pretty early on. Just sometimes . . . I don't know." He trailed off.

"Sometimes what?" I cocked my head.

"I don't really know where I was going with that. Nowhere, I'm sure. Just sometimes—whether it be in marriage or at the firm—I just feel like maybe there should be more. Or maybe I think it should be easier. But I'm thirty-three. I should know better. You know? That doesn't even make any sense, I'm sure."

"No, I really do think I understand." And I think I had pushed him as far as he was going to go, today. "I'm sorry to bring up such a strange topic. Just some self-reflection, I guess. Can I tell you a little more about this case?"

He looked relieved to have a topic change. "Of course."

I launched into my story, reliving the last week of my job. He commented, asked questions, and was engaged. I got him back. Just because he was married—and now admitting it—didn't mean we were doing anything wrong by having a meal and conversation. It was simply about our jobs, our careers. It was innocent.

As we got our bill from the waitress (split, so even more above board than if he offered to pay for it) and pulled out our credit cards, I asked casually, "I don't know if you're ever up for another lunch, but if you are, I'm really okay with it. Or even just a coffee. Doesn't have to be a full meal. I mean, thank you for telling me you're married and all, but I'm still okay with meeting as just friends and kind of business acquaintances. As long as your wife wouldn't have a problem with it, of course."

He looked at me thoughtfully, started to say

something, and cut himself off. Squaring his shoulders, he said, "You know, I think another lunch would be great. I'm sure my wife wouldn't mind. I have business lunches all the time. That's what these feel like."

Okay, that stung a little, but whatever. I was getting what I wanted—finally. "Cool." I tried not to look too pleased with myself. "What day are you thinking?"

I drove home that afternoon, feeling something I couldn't remember feeling in a long time—smug.

Chapter 23

NELLIE

Something was still up with my husband, and I wanted to know what it was. It seemed like we had gone back to normal after all this baby talk and he seemed so happy, but now . . . he was distant again. Did I really have to get pregnant right now to get my husband back? Was he suddenly married to his job? Sure, he was always a hard worker and wasn't afraid of long hours, but he never acted like this. Like he wasn't interested in me. And it was pissing me off. And making me extremely nervous.

Sunday night, I went out to the grocery store to grab a few things. Like more booze to settle my nerves. And blueberry muffins. I was impatiently stalking the aisles, red basket hooked on my arm. Harrison declined going with me, saying he needed to work on a few things at home. Right. He couldn't even come up with a better word than "things." That was not like him. Clearly, something was going on. And I needed to fix it.

I turned to head toward the bakery just as a couple was walking down the aisle, both their hands resting on the cart handle. How cute, I thought sarcastically. I went to step around them, when I realized the guy was Calvin. What the hell?

"Calvin?" I couldn't stop myself from saying in disbelief.

They both looked up, the pretty young girl looking confused, Calvin looking . . . like typical Calvin. "Oh, hey, Nellie. What's up?"

What's up? What's fucking up? What . . . what the fuck?

I hated being caught off guard. "Um, just shopping. You?" I hated saying um.

"Shopping as well. This is my girlfriend, Monique. Monique, this is an old friend from Chicago. Nellie."

Monique reached out for my hand, and I shook hers firmly. My thoughts were racing. Had he had a girlfriend the whole time? Was he just toying with me?

"Oh, do you own the tanning salon?" she asked me in a high-pitched voice.

I forced myself to smile. Potential customer, and all that. "I do. Feel free to drop in sometime. We have beds, spray tans, and custom spray tans with a few of the girls." I reached into my purse automatically and pulled out a business card.

"I will, thank you! I know Calvin has been there and he said it was great." She smiled warmly at me, and I smiled back.

"So happy to hear that. Great meeting you, Monique. And nice to see you, Calvin."

I started to walk away after a head nod, but inside I was seething. I was picking out muffins moments later when I felt a presence next to me.

"Nells?"

I turned sharply. "What the hell, Calvin?"

He smirked. "I'm sorry I wasn't honest with you earlier. Monique and I are pretty serious, and she works out here. I got a job transfer, and we bought a house together. I didn't mean to dupe you, but you were so hysterical freaking out like you did when you saw me. I couldn't resist yanking your chain."

Yanking my chain? I'd been beside myself thinking Calvin moved back here to try to win me back or was going to try to hurt my marriage in some way, and he just thought this was a joke? Before I went off on him, I stopped myself. He was a twenty-two-year-old kid. Fuck him. My marriage was safe. Calvin was in a relationship. I was free.

"You know what? No big deal. She seems really nice, Calvin. Be sure to tell her to come in. And good luck."

"Thanks, Nells. You too. See you around." He gave a friendly wave and was off, his hands shoved in his pockets. I breathed a sigh of relief. I couldn't believe I was off the hook that easily.

* * *

I went to work on Monday morning, my happiness from the run-in with Calvin completely dissipated. I couldn't seduce Harrison last night; he said he was too tired. Then this morning I tried to engage him in conversation over breakfast, and he wouldn't look up from the newspaper. He said he was following some big case at work and needed all his time to focus on that and keep up-to-date on what was happening. Couldn't he have done that at work?

At the salon, Kerri could sense my bad mood and avoided my office in the morning, only dropping by when I was in the bathroom to put a "Starbie" and plain bagel next to my computer. Smart girl. I needed to make sure I gave her a good Christmas bonus.

Just before lunch, Kerri stuck her head in the office. I was blankly staring at schedules, knowing I had to start thinking of the upcoming holidays when scheduling employees, but not reading anything on the screen. "Nellie?"

I jumped, then turned. "Yes?"

"Sorry. Prue is here for her first spray tan. Did you want to chat with her prior to Kara taking her back?"

"Yes, I do. Thank you."

I had spaced Prue was coming in today for a spray tan. With most first-time appointments, I tried to talk to them prior to Kara starting on them, to answer any questions and explain the process and after care—don't shower right away, don't workout, etc. Technically, Kara could do it, but if I was here I preferred it to be me. I had better customer service skills, Kara was better at actually applying the tan. It worked out.

Kerri left my doorway and I took a deep breath, knowing I needed to put on a happy face and smile and get through this consultation. Maybe I could ask Prue for lunch. Maybe I could vent. Wait—was I considering Prue a friend now? I didn't consider anybody friends. Acquaintances—yes. Work associates—yes. Harrison's friends—yes. But not my friends. I didn't have any friends. My last friend was Jemima from high school, and that didn't end well at all. But maybe—maybe there could be a friendship between me and Prue. Maybe I didn't always have to go through life without friends.

I shelved those thoughts to dissect later. Brushing off my clothes, I headed out to the front desk where Prue was waiting in her baggy sweatpants and sweatshirt. With how short she was, she could easily pass as a college student who just rolled out of bed after a long night of partying and threw on the first thing she found. But I couldn't really judge her this time, as I was the one who told her not to wear anything tight. After a spray tan—really nothing felt worse than tight-fitting jeans.

"Hi, Prue," I greeted her with a smile as I approached the reception desk.

"Hi. How's your day?" she asked pleasantly.

"Busy but good. Are you excited for your first spray tan?"

"I am, but a little nervous, too. Mostly just about the being naked in front of a stranger part." She gave a short little laugh, but her eyes looked unsure.

"You'll do fine. Kara is strictly a professional. But let me take you back to the room and I'll go over a few things with you."

We walked down the hallway together and into room 2, one of our three spray tan rooms. This room obviously didn't have a tanning bed in it and instead contained the items needed for a spray tan, plus a large tarp over one section of the wall. The client was to stand on the tarp so the spray tan wouldn't get on the floor or the walls. They wore a cap over their hair to protect their strands, and a tiny pair of thong underwear, but that was it. Some chose not to have the underwear because of tan lines, but Kara also knew how to work around the straps to ensure no tan lines and so that she didn't have to stare at a vagina for thirty minutes. She sometimes liked to joke how she could feel like a gynecologist when she came to work.

Prue opted for the underwear, which I knew she would, and I let her know Kara would come in first to chat with her and talk about the color she wanted before Prue would get undressed. I explained with motions how to hold her arms, how to stand, when she would need to turn around, et cetera, even though Kara would go through this as well. With first-time clients, I liked them to feel as informed as possible going into the appointment.

"When you're finished, Kara will basically blow-dry you. Seriously. With this big fan, she'll help make sure you aren't sticky and wet before you put your clothes back on. When she leaves, you're good to get changed. Don't shower or work out for four to six hours after the spray is on. When you do shower, you'll notice some of the water is brown, and that's totally normal. It's not your spray tan coming off. You can sleep in the spray tan, but I don't really recommend it. Because spray tan does carry a smell, it can come off on your sheets and leave your bed smelling pretty funky."

Prue smiled at that. "Good thing I sleep alone then," she joked.

I smiled. "And that's about it. Do you have any

questions for me?"

She shook her head. "I don't think so. Wait—how long does it last?"

"Usually 7-10 days. You'll see it gradually start to fade after five or so."

"Got it. I think I'm ready!"

"Okay, great. I'll go grab Kara. Enjoy!"

After Kara disappeared inside the room, I sat at the front desk with Kerri, waiting for Prue to get done. She helped me figure out our holiday scheduling. We would be closed Thanksgiving Day but not the day after, and running huge promotions for Black Friday. Then with Christmas, I wanted to close Christmas Eve and Christmas Day, but be open the day after, because it was a Saturday and I could imagine people were going to be out and about.

After about twenty minutes, Prue appeared at the reception desk, looking a little glowy.

"How did it go?" I asked her, looking up from the schedules.

"I think I passed!" she said, smiling at me. "Do you want to grab lunch, Nellie?"

"Sure thing. Let me just grab my coat and purse and I'll be ready. Mediterranean?"

"Sure!"

After a few minutes, we were seated and waiting for our food to come to us.

"This might sound silly, but I don't know if I feel like I look super tan yet. But maybe it's because I'm wearing so many clothes," Prue said, pulling up her sweatshirt sleeves and looking at her arms.

"It will take about an hour or two for you to be able to

notice a difference. And it's fairly gradual, so you won't just look in the mirror and freak out today," I assured her.

"Oh good."

Eric placed our plates down—kabobs for me, another gyro for her, and we dug into our food.

"I feel like I haven't talked to you in a while. What's new?" she asked me.

"Well, I did get some good news actually. The doctor said I'm healthy and we can start trying for a baby anytime. My husband was thrilled."

She paused, her gyro halfway to her mouth. "Really? Wow. That's incredible. That's great. Wow. Do you think you'll start trying soon?"

"If it was up to my husband, I'd already be pregnant by now!" I laughed, popping a pepper into my mouth. "But I'm okay waiting just a little bit longer. I'm a planner by nature. I want all my ducks in a row before I do something as life-changing as becoming someone's mother."

She swallowed, not making eye contact with me. "Well, that's great news then. I'm sure your husband is thrilled."

Didn't I just say that? "Yes, he sure is. But we'll see. His evil mother was basically forcing the appointment on me. I didn't feel like I needed one because it's not like we were having issues or even trying yet, but she insisted." I sighed.

"Do you not get along with her?"

"Oh, she's fine. She's just the classic overbearing mom. My husband is an only child and her only son and all that jazz. Sometimes she makes me feel like I'm not good enough for him or their family. But I try my hardest." That was partially true. In the beginning, I did try. My hardest. Then I just kind of gave up when I realized she was never going to change.

"What a bummer. How does your husband feel about that?"

I considered the question. "I think he tries mostly to stay out of it. I feel bad for him a lot, but usually it's his mom acting like a child, not me. I don't know what I could do different to please her. But don't let me drone on and on about mothers-in-law from hell. Didn't you tell me you had a date? How did it go?"

Her face stayed the same—very neutral, not giving me anything to go off of. "Oh, it went fine. We have a lot in common, but I don't know if it will go anywhere."

"Why not?" I pressed. "You're an attractive girl. You have a good personality. What's the problem? Is it him?"

"I don't really know, for sure. I just don't want to rush into anything too fast, you know? I'm not really in any hurry to settle down again. I don't think."

She sure didn't sound positive about that. "Well, Prue, from what I know about you, it's that you deserve some good to happen in your life. And I really hope you find it." I said that with sincerity, and I had a weird feeling inside as I said it. I really meant it. I liked Prue. I thought she was a good person, and she was kind to me. She did deserve happiness. And I wanted it for her.

"Thanks, Nellie. That's really nice of you to say." She still didn't look at me, just continued to eat her food. Something about her was off. Maybe the date really went that badly. In the words of Prue, that was a bummer.

We finished our lunches quickly and quietly, then

stood to leave.

"I hope you like the finished result. Let me know if you ever want to schedule another one," I said, slipping my long camel-colored coat on.

"Thanks, I will."

We walked toward the door, both waving at Eric as we stepped outside and into the cold.

"You know what? I can't believe I never asked you this, but I don't even think I know your husband's name," Prue said suddenly, as we neared the tanning salon.

I turned to her with surprise. "No? Oh, it's just Harrison. Harrison Hawthorne."

Chapter 24

PRUE

On my next date—meeting? lunch?—with Harrison, he once again wore his wedding ring. I could sense there had been a shift in his demeanor from our first two dates to the third and now the fourth. And I now I knew what the cause of that was.

They were going to start trying for a baby. He couldn't be considering starting something with me or breaking it off with her when a possible baby was on the table.

"I'm so thankful; last week should be the final trial week. Then we get some time off. And it should time out accordingly with the holidays, so I'm happy about that," I said, as I took a sip of my coffee.

"That's excellent. Nothing worse than having to work on Christmas Day," Harrison agreed.

231

"Do you go all out with celebrations?" I asked.

"Nothing too big. Since it's just me and my wife at home, we keep it fairly casual. I mean, we decorate and have a tree and we put lights outside—mostly just to keep up with the neighborhood—but on Christmas Day we go to my parents' house and spend some time there. I'm an only child and she doesn't have any family, so our celebrations are pretty tame."

"Wow. Your wife doesn't have any family? That's really sad."

"It is. Her father died when she was young and her mother about ten years ago. Cancer."

Something niggled at me. Her mother died of cancer? I thought Nellie mentioned a house fire when it came to her mother.

"Very sad. Luckily, she has your family now. That's got to be great for her."

He grimaced a little, looking down at his burger. "Yeah. Except, her and my mom don't always see eye to eye. They both have very strong but different personalities."

I nodded sympathetically. "That must be tough then. Especially with you being an only child."

"It definitely presents its challenges. But what about you? How do you celebrate?"

"Oh, my mom and I usually do something together. You know about my dad, but Mom and I make sure to do something nice on the holidays together. We always will visit his grave, and then we try to do something fun. Sometimes it's a little mini-trip, sometimes it's a football game, but we just like to be together during that time.

We're very close," I tacked on at the end.

"That sounds wonderful." He smiled at me, and I felt my heart lift a little. I tried to ignore the other feelings—unpleasant feelings—that tried to bubble to the surface. I tried to remember my mother's words—I deserved happiness. And I did.

The following week when I met with Harrison, he seemed in a different mood. Quiet, almost a little stormy.

"Is everything okay?" I ventured to ask, figuring it was something with his job.

"Yeah. Yeah, everything is fine. Just fine," he muttered, balling up his napkin and throwing it on the table, then picking it back up and starting to shred it.

"Okay." I sat quietly, unsure how to handle this situation. "I'm happy to listen, if you need a set of ears to vent to. Or help you figure something out."

He looked up at me then. "I'm sorry, I'm probably not being very good company, am I?" He rolled his shoulders. "But it's personal . . ."

Meaning it had to do with his wife, his marriage. I had to tread carefully. "Oh, I understand. That's all right. What did you think of the snow a few days ago? That was crazy."

I got him talking on a new subject, and then after our food came and we were quiet once again, I tried my hand. "I know it's none of my business really, but I hope things improve for you. I mean, I have no idea what's going on really, but I definitely hope it's all okay."

He smiled at me, seeming to be more relaxed after eating. "Thanks for saying that. I guess I'm just getting frustrated because I really want a baby and my wife keeps holding out. And I have no idea why. It seems the perfect time to try, but I think she's worried about her body or something. She's really into fitness, but that shouldn't stop someone from creating a family."

The hairs on my arms rose slightly. I nodded and tried to look wise. "I'm sure it has to be quite challenging on the woman. Her body will change and probably never be the same. If your wife really loves fitness, that's probably really hard for her to accept."

He looked at me thoughtfully. "That's a really good point. I guess I didn't think of all that."

I tried to cover my tracks. "But at the same time, when does it become unhealthy to your marriage? Having children is a huge deal and if the husband and wife can't see eye to eye on that, it can become problematic."

He nodded again. "I agree. I just—I don't know what to do. I've always wanted children and I thought she did, too. I don't know what the sudden hold up is."

I reflected on past conversations. Didn't she say she wanted children? She even went to the doctor to find out if she was healthy and in good shape. Yes, she said it was at the insistence of her mother-in-law, but she never said anything about not wanting children. Just that she was a planner and needed a little more time to figure everything out. I knew she liked fitness—it was evident by her body— but she never told me that was the reason why she wasn't trying for kids.

I thought back to past conversations with Harrison. It seemed that what he was telling me sometimes contradicted what she was telling me. So who was lying? I could bet it wasn't Harrison. But why was she? I vowed then to find out all I could about Nellie. I sensed something was off a few weeks ago, but now . . . something was definitely fishy in her world. And I was going to uncover it.

We finished up and the waitress soon took our plates away, setting down one bill without asking us if we wanted separate checks. Harrison picked it up and reached for his wallet.

"Oh, I can get my half," I said, reaching for my purse.

He waved me away. "It's all right. I feel bad for unloading on you like that. This can be my penance."

I shook my head. "Don't feel bad about it. We all have our problems. Heck, I told you all my baggage weeks ago. And you didn't make me pay for lunch!"

"Maybe next time then. It will be a makeup penance for you."

He smiled at me and I got a little shiver. Next time . . . and he was paying for my lunch. Slow and steady.

"Sounds good."

We got up and started walking for the door. I don't know what came over me, I was already feeling like a monster from our conversation, but I felt some sick urge to ask, "I'm sorry, I don't even think I asked your wife's name."

"You didn't? Oh, it's Nellie. Nellie Hawthorne."

Chapter 25

NELLIE

"Harrison, do you want to have lunch today?" I asked my husband, just as we were getting ready to walk out into the snowy weather and into our cars.

He turned to me, surprise on his face. "Lunch?"

"We never have lunch together. I recently started taking actual lunch breaks and I think they're really helping. I thought maybe we could go together."

He cleared his throat. "I have a meeting during lunch today. What about tomorrow?"

I thought for a moment. "And I have some interviews scheduled then. Maybe Thursday?"

He looked relieved. "Yes, Thursday sounds good. Lunch it is."

"Okay, great." Our conversation felt stilted, but I turned my lips up for a kiss, just in time to see Harrison turn his back to me and keep walking toward his car. Ouch.

I stewed silently on my way to work. Harrison had never made me feel this way in all our years of marriage. I didn't know what to do. I didn't think he was not to be trusted, but did I have to start looking through his phone, breaking into his email? What if something was going on? What if he wanted to leave me? I was Nellie Hawthorne. I didn't know how to be anyone else.

I kept my head down and worked hard that day, dealing with Christmas promotions, conducting two interviews for new staff members. We had one front desk girl quit unexpectedly and one that was going to be traveling through most of December and January, so we needed replacements ASAP for them. I tried to ignore the nagging feeling that something was really wrong with Harrison. That something was wrong with us.

But what could it be? I was putting my all into us right now. I was trying to be the perfect wife, the perfect woman for him. I was bending over backward trying to do right. I was trying to get along with his mom. I was going out for business dinners. I was wearing the clothes I knew he liked and the perfume he bought me last Christmas. What? What more could I do?

The following day, I had lunch with Prue. I had really started to think of her as my only friend and was hoping she could offer me some insight or advice.

"You okay?" she asked me straightaway. I clearly wasn't hiding my feelings.

I puffed out a breath. "I don't think so. My husband is acting so strange these days. I feel like there's a huge disconnect between us, and I don't know why."

She looked closely at me. "Why do you think that?"

"He just doesn't seem interested in me at all. He's always on his phone or his computer or at the office. He's always been a busy guy—hell, I'm busy myself—but we've always made time for one another. We went through this a few months ago, both just so busy, but then things got better. I don't know why it's gone back to that again. And it's not like he's mean to me, it's just like he's lost interest in me. This feels different from before. And I don't know how to fix it now!"

Her eyes widened. "Whoa. I'm sorry to hear that. You don't have any idea what could be causing it?"

I thought over her words. "There's only one thing I could think of but . . . I don't know." Did I really want to divulge about Calvin? Could Prue be trusted? But it wasn't like she was in our circle. She wasn't a neighbor or co-worker of Harrison's. She was a nobody, really.

"What?" she urged. "Even if it's something small, at least it's something to go off of."

I took a deep breath. "I'm going to tell you something in confidence. Can I have your trust? Please?"

She took a breath, and I saw her swallow deeply. "Okay," she said, her voice a little shaky.

I took a deep breath myself, still unsure that I was really going to do this. But Prue could help me. She could help me get out of this mess.

"I—I was having an affair. Years ago. Before we were married." I felt a small weight lift off my chest and felt like that was a good sign. "I'm worried maybe Harrison found out somehow. The guy actually just moved here from Chicago." I saw her eyes widen. "Not because of me or anything. He actually has a girlfriend and they are serious and buying a house here and all that. It's just a coincidence. But him showing up here really threw me. I keep worrying Harrison somehow found out, but I don't know how he could have. But I can't think of anything else." I finally looked up, and noticed Prue looked a little pale. This news was hitting her hard. I knew I portrayed myself as the woman who has it all and who definitely had her shit together. This was probably shocking for her.

"Wow. Nellie, I . . . I wasn't expecting that. I thought maybe you would say something about the baby stuff but . . . jeez. Wow."

Fuck! The baby thing. Why didn't I think of that? That would have been so much better than me blabbing a huge secret like that. Damn it! What was wrong with me? I always had everything planned out, I was always one step ahead of the game. What was happening to me?

"I guess maybe that could be a part of it, but probably not. We've agreed to wait a few months until after the holidays to start getting baby on the brain again," I said smoothly.

Her eyebrows flickered. "Oh. I see. That's good you've decided on that. Together." She was speaking in short sentences, clearly still overwhelmed.

I bit my lower lip. "Do you think I'm an awful person?" I asked in a hushed voice. "You can tell me the truth."

"What? No! No, I don't think you're a horrible person, Nellie. I mean, we all do bad things, right? And this is really over?"

"For years, Prue. Honestly. I kind of freaked out

before the wedding because I was scared of commitment. I saw Calvin—that's his name—for a few months and actually thought of calling off the wedding because I didn't think I could do the whole commit yourself to one person for the rest of your life thing. But I broke it off with him three weeks before the wedding, and I've never cheated ever again. I'm one hundred percent in my marriage and have been from the moment I said my vows. But I never told Harrison. And I got so scared thinking he would find out."

"And if he did find out . . . ?"

"He would leave me. I know he would. He wouldn't stand for that. Even though it was before we were married, it's still cheating. It's still wrong. But I don't want to lose him. I know I wasn't a good person before. I was letting myself go down the wrong path with Calvin, just like I had always done, but I'm better than that now. I'm a better person than that. I know I am." I felt that strange sensation in my eyes again, like I wanted to cry. I pushed the feeling down. "But I don't want to lose my husband. He's all I have. Literally. He's the only person who's saved me from . . . me, so many times. I can't lose him." I said this last part in a whisper, feeling totally overwhelmed at the idea of losing Harrison, my lifeline. It just wasn't an option.

Prue sat back in her chair, still kind of staring at me with the oddest expression on her face. Suddenly, I knew what this was about. She didn't want to be my friend anymore. Prue was—what did she always call herself?—the quintessential good girl. The good girl was not friends with the bad girl, the evil girl. The woman who cheated on her perfectly wonderful fiancé because they were scared to say

"I do." Harrison would never do something like what I did to him. Fuck, Harrison was the quintessential good guy. They would make a perfect match. How did I end up with him? Oh yeah . . . by lying. Because that's all I did.

"I'm sorry. You think I'm awful. And I am. I know it. But I'm trying to be better, Prue. Really, I am." I felt the tears again push against my eyelids and decided to just roll with it. Why bother pushing it away? This could be the first big change I make. Actually crying. It felt weird.

"Nellie. I just . . . I honestly don't know what to say. I'm a little caught off guard, yes. But you can't think of yourself as a horrible person. Honestly. You made a mistake. Should you tell Harrison? I don't know. Would it help or hurt? I don't know . . . It's so complicated . . . and I've never been married. I don't know how to give good advice here. I'm sorry. I feel like I'm failing you."

Impulsively, I reached across the table and grabbed Prue's hand. "Thank you for just listening to me. It really means a lot. I've never had someone to talk about this stuff with. I was worried at first about telling you and I didn't want you to think I'm awful but I'm glad I did. I don't need advice right now. I just needed a listener. And now I'm babbling. I'm sorry."

We both laughed, and I noticed then she had tears in her eyes, too. Wow. I had really moved her.

This was a big thing.

"Thanks for telling me, Nellie. It makes me really understand everything so much more. And I'm here to help you. Don't you worry."

Chapter 26

PRUE

"Miss Prue!"

I walked over to the table where little kindergartener Ellie was waving her hand around wildly.

"Do you need something?" I asked, bending down to her level.

"My fork fell through my pants."

I looked down, and sure enough, the metal fork was through her thin gray pants, four little holes showing where each prong was. She removed the fork and grinned at me, brandishing the silverware like it was a weapon.

"Um . . . how did a fork get in your pants?" I asked, not sure what to make of this situation.

"I dropped it and it just fell in my pants!" she said in her high-pitched voice with a slight lisp.

"Nu uh! She wanted the fork to go through her pants.

She no drop it," Camden said, sitting to the right of Ellie. Ellie glared at him.

"Ellie, did you purposely put the fork in your pants?" I asked, in my sternest voice even though I really wanted to laugh.

She looked at me with serious eyes and nodded.

"And why would you do that?"

"I just . . . I just wanted to see what would happen." Her voice was now small, and she dropped her eyes to her pants.

"Well, now you have to spend the rest of the day with holes in your pants. And your mom and dad probably aren't going to be very happy you ruined a pair of pants, now are they?"

"Are you going to tell them?"

I cocked my head. "I don't need to tell them. They'll see the holes right away."

"Shoot!" she exclaimed. "I'm gonna be in soooo much trouble."

Funny, she didn't sound too tore up over that news. I shook my head and kept walking, just as my mom entered into the lunchroom. It was December 22 and the final day of school before winter break started. We were expected to get a huge snowstorm—a foot of snow was predicated—and it had already started falling outside. I couldn't wait to get home and snuggle up with Clemmie and not have to worry about going anywhere. I had chicken noodle soup in the crock pot, a fully stocked kitchen thanks to my massive grocery store trip earlier this week when the storm was announced, and all the *Gilmore Girls* seasons on Netflix. A foot of snow? I wasn't scared!

"Hey, Mom." I walked over to her.

"Hi, dear. We're going to dismiss school early today," she informed me.

"Oh really? Is it getting bad out?"

"It is. And while it's not terrible right at this moment, by three o'clock it's supposed to be nearly un-travelable out there. So we'll dismiss at one to try to ensure everyone gets home safely."

"Gotcha. Do you want me to stay a little later today and help out?"

"If you could, that would be great. I know there will be chaos with the change."

I had been subbing all this week, as Maisy was on a tropical vacation with her family through the New Year. It had been fun to get back in the groove of the school. Our case was officially wrapped at work, so my schedule was finally back to normal. And thankfully. I didn't mind being slower around Christmas time.

Mom clapped her hands three times to get the kindergarten's class attention. "Hello, kindergarten friends!"

"Hi, Mrs. Doherty," they chorused back in their sweetest little voices. I smirked.

"Do you see all the snow outside?" she asked, and everybody turned toward the window, their heads bobbing up and down. "Because of the weather we're going to dismiss school early today. You'll go out to recess like normal after lunch, then when you come in your teachers will help you get ready to leave. The buses will be lined up like usual and many of your parents are coming to get you today, okay? Your teachers will have more instructions for each of you when you get back inside. We'll see you back here in two weeks, and have a happy holiday!"

There was a plethora of voices that shouted back to their beloved principal, and Mom took some time to walk around the room and chat with a few individuals and dole out hugs. I smiled watching her. Mom had been in education my whole life, starting out as a teacher, then assistant principal, then six years ago taking over as Principal at Eakwood Elementary. I was happy she loved her career so much.

After the kindergarten class left, we still had two more classes to get through, then I helped with the early dismissal procedures. It was a flurry of activity, with an unplanned early out on the last day of school before a two-week break. Utter madness was a nice way of putting it.

After the last student was safely picked up and driven away from the school, I followed Mom back into her office.

"Are you sticking around here for long?" I asked her, while peering out her office window. "You probably won't want to wait to get on the road."

"I'll be gone within fifteen minutes," she told me, sitting behind her desk. "Are you sure you don't want to stay at my house tonight? What if it gets so bad you won't be able to come over for Christmas?"

"Mom, I'm sure the snow will be cleared in the next three days. And if not—you're not that far. Clem and I can walk to you."

"Prudence Camilla Doherty! You will not be walking outside in a foot of snow just to come to my house."

"Mom, it was just a joke! But really, I'm sure by Christmas Eve I'll be able to drive over, and I will. But I still have a lot to do around the house tonight. I'll be okay. Are you sure you have everything you need?"

I worried about Mom being alone, and often suggested she get a dog or even a cat to keep her company, but she always insisted she was just fine by herself.

"Oh yes, dear. I'll be fine. I just worry about you. I'm your mother. And speaking of . . . is there anything you want to tell me?"

"About what?"

"Your last date."

I could feel myself blush. "Not really much to tell. It was good."

"I've lost track of how many dates you've been on."

I shrugged. "I haven't really kept track."

"And your next date is?"

"Mom, really?"

She gazed at me. "I can't ask my daughter when her next date with a man she is smitten with is? And can I also ask when I will finally get to meet him?"

Yeah right. "There's simply not that much to tell you, Mom. I don't know if things are getting serious or not. So if I can't tell, I think that means they probably aren't."

She continued to hold my gaze. "I don't know who you are trying to fool, dear Prue. I know there is more to this story than you are letting on. When you're ready to talk about it, I'll be here. And I hope it's sooner than later. For your sake."

* * *

Of course. Mom had to know who Harrison Hawthorne was. She had to know he was a married man. The question was—why had she not called me out on it yet? To let me make my own mistake? Or maybe she didn't know or thought Harrison was separated? I didn't know for sure, but I knew I couldn't tell her the real story yet. I was too embarrassed to admit what I was doing.

Mom's words continued to echo in my head as I carefully maneuvered my car home. The streets were already getting bad, the snow was piling on thick, and the wind was causing it to blow, diminishing visibility. What was usually a five-minute drive took me nearly thirty minutes, and I passed one accident and a car in the ditch on my way home.

I walked inside and removed my coat, hat, and gloves, realizing I had started sweating somewhere along my drive. Feeling icky, I decided to shower after letting Clemmie outside.

As I let the hot water wash over me, not wanting to get out and succumb to the cold again, I let my mind wander to Harrison. Exactly what kind of game was I playing? When would it end? And who would come out victorious?

After my shower, I sat on the couch with Clem curled up at my side, turning on the TV and navigating to Netflix. After one episode of *Gilmore Girls*, my phone dinged with a new text message.

Harrison: *This snow is no joke, huh?*

I smiled. *It's not. Are you home?*

I am. Sounds like most of the city will be shut down tomorrow.

Ah. So that's why he was texting. *So reschedule?*

I think we'll have to. Maybe next week?

My heart sank a little, but I understood. If everything was closed, where would we meet? And what would he tell her? It made sense, even if I didn't like it.

Sure. Tuesday? Lunch?

How about dinner? I'll make up having to cancel on you.

It's not your fault this weather is insane.

I still feel bad. And I was looking forward to it.

I paused for a moment, letting his words sink over me. *Me too. And dinner sounds great.*

Good. Keep warm. And Merry Christmas.

Merry Christmas.

I closed my phone and resumed the next episode but couldn't pay attention to the loveable mother-daughter duo and their fiery dynamic. I could only think of Harrison, Harrison Hawthorne, the man that was consuming my thoughts as of late. I was disappointed we had to reschedule our date, but everything became a lot trickier when your love interest happened to be married.

As Lorelai and Rory Gilmore struggled through another family dinner with Lorelai's awful mother and stoic father, I thought about my situation. How did I get here? And how did I get out of it?

I couldn't go to my mother yet with the full story. I was ashamed of what I was doing with Harrison, but really, what was I doing? Going out on a few dates. Exchanging a few chaste kisses on the cheeks. One night we held hands as he walked me to my door, though I will admit I was the one that had reached for his hand. But he didn't let go. We had yet to have a proper kiss. We certainly hadn't slept together. It was all very above board. He was married.

And his wife considered me a friend.

I didn't know how I let this happen. I didn't know who he was when I first met him the past summer on our walks. I also didn't know who Nellie was when I started tanning regularly. After Harrison told me his name and the firm he worked at, I googled him. I didn't realize it the first time I cyber stalked him, but as we talked more I did more searches on him and eventually found his wife. By that time, Nellie and I had already started talking, and the wheels were in motion. The chain of events were already starting to spiral out of control before I could connect all the dots. But even once I found out Harrison was married —and I had regular coffee and lunch dates with his wife—I didn't stop seeing him. Or wanting him. As I learned more about Nellie, one thing was clear to me—she was not meant for Harrison. How those two got together, how they got married, and how they were still married—I didn't understand. And once she admitted her affair, even though it was in the past—that was the last straw. Harrison was a good man. I had tried to drop casual hints about taking our friendship to a new level, and he was polite and kind when turning down my thinly veiled advances. But he didn't stop seeing me either.

I'd also come to realize Nellie was a pathological liar. I'd started catching her, several times. It was like she couldn't keep her stories straight, but the closer we got, the more distracted she had started to become. It was like she wanted me to know who she really was. I didn't understand why, and didn't care. But I couldn't let on what I knew about her husband and that it was me he was texting at four o'clock on a Tuesday. Keep your friends close and your enemies closer. I couldn't show my hand yet. I didn't have my plan fully figured out yet. I just knew Nellie was a bad person, and I did not want to see someone like her win. She didn't deserve to. Harrison didn't deserve it.

And I didn't deserve it. I deserved to be happy. For once. I deserved the cards to fall in my favor. And even if I had to shuffle them a few which ways, I was determined to get there. Somehow. Some way.

Chapter 27

NELLIE

Christmas Eve. A time to be thankful. To be with family. To feel love and peace and joy. And instead, I was crying in the bathroom. Me. Crying. Again! This was seriously fucked up. And I hated it. I hated what was happening to my life, that it was spinning out of control and I wasn't at the helm. I wasn't calling the shots. I wasn't pulling the strings.

I looked in the mirror, wincing at what I saw back. Mascara down my cheeks. Eyes puffy. Hair tangled and ratty. I needed to get it together. I had a chance to get the upper hand back. And by all means, I was going to do whatever it took. I had been through enough shit in my life. I deserved to be happy, dammit. I had paid my dues. A plenty.

I heard Harrison enter the bedroom through the en suite door and quickly splashed water on my face. When I couldn't get the mascara to rub off my cheeks (why could it leave my lashes so freely, yet not my goddamn face) I used a makeup remover wipe to take off all my makeup, then cleansed my face. The lavender scent helped calm me, helped me see a little clearer.

I straightened my spine and looked in the mirror again. Much better. I grabbed my paddle brush and combed out my locks, then spritzed a shine spray into them. Even better. Okay.

I opened the door to see Harrison standing by the bed, smiling at his cell phone. I got it. Clearly, something was going on with Harrison. Was it another woman? Probably. What else could it possibly be? I was a cheater, I knew the signs. The later nights. Always on his phone. No longer leaving his cell around the house; it was always in his pocket now. But it was something that he was that I wasn't when I was with Calvin—happy. He was happier. Whoever the hell this bitch was, she was making him happy. With Calvin, I was mostly just satisfied. But not happy.

The odd thing was, he never smelt of another woman. And I checked. I went through his clothes, smelled his shirts, looked for lipstick marks on his tie. Nothing. When I hugged him when he walked in the door, he smelled like his usual self. I didn't see any scratch marks on his back or hickies on his neck—not that I really thought he would be that obvious. But it was weird. Either he was better at covering up than I ever thought he could be or . . . maybe it wasn't an affair. Maybe I was wrong.

I pushed those thoughts aside for the time being. "Hi," I said.

He looked up, seemingly startled. "Oh, hi. I didn't know you were in there."

I made myself smile. "How is it out there?"

Harrison had been outside to snow blow our sidewalk. We normally had a company do it, but Harrison didn't have them come around the holidays. Usually the time when we had snow, plus company, so it was about the worst time to lay them off, but he said he enjoyed the physical activity it gave him. As long as I didn't have to help, so be it.

"It's pretty awful." His cheeks still looked pink from being out in the cold, and his hair was flattened funny around his head from his hat. "So much snow. The drifts are probably four feet high, if not more."

I shook my head as I crossed the room. "That's just insane. But nothing like a White Christmas, huh? It does look pretty. If only it wasn't so cold." I was looking out the window, rubbing my hands up and down my arms as if I was standing outside and feeling the biting temperatures.

"Yeah. Hey, I'm going to hop in the shower, okay?"

"Want me to join you?" I leaned seductively into him, kissing him on the neck.

He pulled away, and my spirits sank. "I just need to wash off the sweat, really. Should be less than five minutes."

"Oh, okay. Well, I'll go get dinner ready, okay? And then I have an early Christmas present to give you."

He looked puzzled. "What? What do you mean?"

I smiled teasingly at him. "Go take that shower, then meet me in the kitchen."

He gave me another confused glance, then strolled in

the bathroom. I heard the water turn on, then made my way into the kitchen, going over what I was going to say when he joined me. If he wasn't excited for my gift, I would know something was really, really wrong. But something told me he would be excited. Or maybe it was just wishful thinking.

I puttered around the kitchen, making sure to put phase one of my announcement into play. I poured myself a glass of strawberry lemonade from the container, leaving the pitcher in the center of the table. I heard the water shut off and at least knew he wasn't kidding about taking a short shower. A few minutes later, he entered the kitchen, dressed but with wet hair. I was seated at the table, hands folded in front of me.

"So what's going on?" he asked, looking at me. "Is that lemonade?"

"Yes. Do you want a glass?" I rose out of my chair, but he held a hand up. "I can get it, thanks. So I'm confused. I mean, I have your Christmas gifts ready to go, but I thought we would do it in the morning, like we usually do."

"Can you sit down?"

His face seemed to pale, but he steadily poured the pink liquid into a glass. "Is everything all right?"

"Oh yes. It's good news. At least, I think so."

"Okay then." He took a seat across from me, took a quick drink, and then looked squarely at me. "What is it?"

I took a deep breath. "I've been doing a lot of thinking lately. A lot of soul searching. Thinking about my life, my career, our marriage. And I know it's taken a little bit of persuading on my end, but I know what's right for us right now. And I'm ready. I'm ready to try for a baby, Harrison.

I'm ready to be a mom."

I watched my husband's reaction closely. I didn't think he could have been more surprised than if I had told him I was already pregnant. Well, maybe not that far, but he was clearly shocked. I sat frozen, waiting for some sort of indication from him. When I saw his smile stretch from ear to ear, I knew I was in the clear. Harrison was back.

"What? You are? Really? How? Really, Nellie?" He jumped up from the chair and over to me, kneeling in front of me with his hands in my mine. "You're really sure?"

"I'm really sure, babe. I've been being so silly. If I constantly try to wait until the exact right moment, the exact perfect timing, it could be forever. And that's not fair to either of us. I don't think there is a perfect moment when it comes to this situation, honestly. But the perfect moment will be when we get the news that we'll be parents."

"But our lives will be changed. Forever."

I nodded. "I know. And they would be changed for the better. Imagine. Us, parents. Mom and Dad. It will be the most incredible job we'll ever do."

Harrison kissed me hard and deep, and I knew then with absolute certainty, if there was anyone else on the side, they were over. Done. Finished. Fuck off, bitch. My husband was back.

"Wow. I'm so happy, Nellie. Thank you. Thank you for being so understanding lately. With my mom and the doctor appointment, and now just being open to this. We get to try for a baby. A baby! I couldn't have asked for a better Christmas gift. I love you so much. I hope you know that."

I wrapped my arms around him, feeling a ton of pressure fall off me. My life was back on track. And if I had to pop out a kid to keep our marriage intact and Harrison happy, then so fucking be it. Bring on the babies. Being worried we wouldn't stay together was silly. My fears of turning out like my own mother were plain dumb. I would do whatever it took to make my marriage work and stay in this life. I would never abandon a child like how my mom left me. And if Harrison thought he could easily replace me, he was wrong. I played for keeps.

"I love you, too. So much. Now, what do you say we get to practicing?" I asked, kissing his neck again. This time, he didn't turn me down.

Game. Set. Match.

Chapter 28

PRUE

Tonight was my dinner date with Harrison, and I had made a decision. After dinner, I was going to invite him back to my place. Sure, it was a small apartment, but I couldn't be embarrassed about it. He knew my situation. It wasn't like I was holding anything back from him. I could ask him over for a nightcap and ask if he wanted to see Clemmie. He hadn't seen her in weeks, since we stopped walking outside. And then . . . we would see where the night would take us. Maybe, if it went to a new level, I could ask him what he thought about us. I didn't want to be the other woman, but in this situation, I could be. It was clear his marriage would implode one day. One day very soon.

Speaking of . . . I glanced at the clock and saw it was nearly noon. Before my date tonight with Harrison Hawthorne, I had a lunch date with Nellie Hawthorne. My life had suddenly become very strange.

It was three days after Christmas, and the snow we were slammed with just before the holiday still lingered. Temperatures struggled to get above twenty, so the snow stayed frozen in place. It really did look like a winter wonderland around these parts.

After putting Clem back into her kennel with a toy, I bundled up and walked out to my car. I once again thought about renting a garage or buying an automatic starter for my car. Now that would come in handy during winter in Illinois. The drive to the restaurant didn't take too long, as the roads were pretty quiet.

I drummed my fingers on the steering wheel, thinking of how this meeting with Nellie would go. I had asked her several more questions about her affair, essentially posing as a concerned friend. And she was buying it. I had never been the manipulator in my life, had never lied like this to anyone before. But when my guilty conscience tried to get the better of me, I reminded myself of who Nellie really was. She was the liar, the manipulator, the cheater. She was in the wrong. I was only protecting Harrison from who he really married, which was essentially a monster. I couldn't believe how many people she had deceived in her path. Or how the fates had aligned and chosen me to be the one she would break down to.

I walked inside and she was already seated, looking at her phone. What did we do when we had to wait before cell phones? Stare into space? It was a novel thought.

"Hi!" I said brightly, approaching the table.

She looked up from her phone and smiled. "Hi, Prue! How are you? How was your Christmas?"

"It was good, thanks." I removed my winter gear and sat down across from her. The waiter came by and I ordered a Coke. "How about yourself?"

"It was wonderful." Her cheeks were glowing, and she looked happy. I felt a knot of fear suddenly.

"Oh yeah?" I asked, trying to keep the wariness out of my voice.

"I have some good news to share," she continued, and I felt the knot grow bigger. Was she . . . was it possible she was . . . ?

"Harrison and I trying for a baby!" she squealed, looking downright thrilled with herself.

I felt my mouth drop open. I hoped I didn't look too horrified. "Say what now? You're trying for a baby?" I felt a little numb.

"Yep! Actively trying, if you know what I'm saying." She wiggled her eyebrows at me and I thought I might get sick. What the hell?

"I . . . wow. I just . . . I think I'm speechless!" I tried to give a little laugh, but it felt hollow to my ears. Where had this come from?

She threw her head back and laughed. She seemed so . . . happy. How was this possible? "I know, right? I was so worried having a baby would change things a lot and maybe not for the better. And I'm talking more than just my body. But it's just—it's the right thing to do. Harrison really wants to be a father. And it will be a good thing."

"So are you doing this only to make Harrison happy? You need to be happy, too." I was trying to find anything I could to talk her out of this. Harrison couldn't have a baby with this wretched person. He would be stuck with her—

forever.

"Well, at first I was kind of thinking of just doing it for him. But I'm happy with the decision. And it makes me even happier seeing how happy he is. Really. It's a good thing." She peered at me. "Are you okay? I'm sorry, is this upsetting you? With your situation and . . ."

"No," I snapped, and she looked startled. "Sorry, no. Like I said, it's just a big surprise. So—are you not telling him about Calvin?"

She looked as though I had slapped her. "What? No. No, I'm not." A strange looked passed over her eyes. "Why would you want me to do that?"

"It's not that I want you to. Just last time you mentioned . . ." I trailed off, unsure where I was going with this. "Sorry, don't listen to me. It's just a lot. But congratulations. And good luck. I wish you both a lot of happiness." The words physically hurt me to say. Where did this leave Harrison and me? Would he want to keep seeing me? I couldn't imagine he would. He was one of the most above-board people I had ever met. If his wife was about to give him the biggest gift of all, why would he leave her? Why would he continue with me? He wouldn't. And I knew it.

Nellie leaned back in her seat and regarded me cautiously. "Thanks. That means a lot to me."

We ate in silence for a few more moments, before she piped up again. "Maybe we could have you over for dinner sometime. I would love for you to meet my husband."

I looked up sharply. She was staring at me, her green eyes piercing. What was with the edge in her voice? And there was no way I could ever set foot in her house—their house. To pretend to meet Harrison for the first time, look over their belongings, their wedding photos. Watch them interact together. There was simply no way.

"Oh, thanks for the invite." I tried my hardest to get my lips to curve up. "Maybe. Let me know when you're thinking and I can check my schedule."

"How about tonight?"

"Tonight?" I nearly choked on my soup. "I'm going to my mom's tonight."

"Ah. Tomorrow?"

I racked my brain. Something was going on. Nellie's whole demeanor had changed. Did she figure us out, right then and there? But how could she possibly know?

"Tomorrow?" My thoughts buzzed. "I have plans with a friend from work. Linds. Going into Chicago."

She nodded curtly. "How about Friday? Maybe this could get us out of Friday night dinner with his family. And you told me earlier you didn't have any plans this weekend. Surely you could make Friday. You could even bring your dog."

She made it sound like I was so pathetic I had to have a dog as my date. Something was definitely wrong here. I had to call Harrison. And soon.

"Friday? Um, yeah. Friday could work." What else could I say? I had already mentioned I had no plans for the entire weekend. I couldn't get out of this one.

She smiled, showing off her straight, perfect teeth. "Wonderful. Friday it is. I can't wait for you to meet my husband."

I smiled back weakly. Trouble was coming.

Chapter 29

NELLIE

Something was off about Prue, and I was going to figure it out. She changed each and every time I brought up Harrison. And what was with her flippant comment about my affair? I stressed to her how important it was that it stay between us, and she just casually mentioned it in conversation? I had to get that figured out, and ASAP. I felt suddenly like I didn't have the upper hand with her, and I didn't like it one fucking bit.

This was my penance for trying to be a good person. The one time I try to befriend someone and have a real friendship with them, something turns out dodgy. But I just couldn't believe that Prue was involved in something shady with Harrison. It wasn't like her. It definitely wasn't like him. So how did the puzzle pieces connect?

Once at home, I did something I had never done

before—went through Harrison's things. I looked in the pockets of his work pants lying on the laundry room floor. I searched through his suit jacket pockets hanging in the closet. I went into his email account on the home laptop (the password was saved so no need for guessing games) and went through his emails, his sent emails, his archived emails, his folders. Nothing.

I thought a few weeks ago that possibly Harrison was seeing someone else. And Prue mentioned she had a date a few weeks ago, but then said nothing else since then. But how could they have met? Where would they have met? Is that why Prue even became my friend, because she knew Harrison was my husband? But then why would she be my friend? And Harrison—he wasn't the guy to cheat. I knew that. Even while I was wading through his emails and looking in his pockets, I knew he wasn't the type of guy to step out on his wife. But I couldn't ignore my gut instinct. Something was wrong here. I just needed to fit all the pieces together.

And fast. I couldn't get pregnant at a time like this. Or . . . why couldn't I? Say Harrison was seeing Prue, or maybe not Prue, maybe just someone else. What if he did want to leave me for her? Harrison would not leave me if I was pregnant. Not a fucking chance. This baby, this miraculous way that I could suddenly conceive again, may just be the thing to hold my marriage together. It would be my golden ticket to staying in the game with Harrison and the Hawthorne family. Why the hell was I so freaked out over a baby before? I might have finally convinced myself I wanted a baby for real this time, but it was also the perfect solution. Harrison would never leave his pregnant wife. If anything shady was going on. And that was a big if.

I heard the front door open and quickly exited out of the email account, shutting down the laptop. I walked to the front hallway and found Harrison removing all his winter gear, a bit of snow still sitting on top of his hat.

"Hi, babe," I said, moving in to give him a kiss.

He shrugged out of his coat and then wrapped his arms around me. "Hi, love. How was your day?"

"It was good. Busy, but good. How was yours?"

He held my hand as we walked into the kitchen. I could get used to this. Now, how to bring up Prue and her coming to dinner? I really hadn't mentioned much about her to him, though I didn't really know why. It was like I was trying to keep the friendship in a bubble or something. I had mentioned lunches with friends but never elaborated, and I assumed he thought I meant my employees or something. So this should be interesting. And I had to watch his reaction closely when I mentioned her name.

"Busy. But good." He smiled at me as he repeated my words. "And I'm starving. How about we start dinner a little early?"

"Sounds fine by me. What are you thinking?"

He started opening cupboards and taking items out. "I bought some ingredients to make homemade pizza. Okay by you?"

"Sure thing. What can I do?"

"Just let me know what you want on your half."

"Light on the cheese and sauce, and with veggies, please."

I took a seat at the table and watched him gather all the ingredients. The pizza crust. Sauce. Bags of veggies for me, including green peppers and mushrooms. Meats for him, like sausage and pepperoni. He worked quickly and efficiently. Harrison didn't love cooking, but he had about three dishes that he loved to make, and pizza was one of them.

"So, have I mentioned to you my new friend that I met through the tanning salon?" I started off with.

He didn't turn around, just kept loading more sauce onto the crust and then swirling it around. "I don't think so."

"Oh. Silly me. We had a client come in pretty frequently and I started chatting with her one day and we seemed to hit it off pretty well."

That got him to turn around. "Really? That's terrific." I could hear the surprise in his voice. I didn't really befriend anyone. I got it.

"Yeah. It's like, we're actually pretty different, but somehow we just clicked. We actually went for lunch once and couldn't stop talking, so we've had a few more lunch dates. She's really cool."

He had gone back to work on the pizza. "That's really awesome, babe. I love hearing that."

"Thanks. And I thought it might be fun to have her over here for dinner some night. Kind of like a thank you for being a regular client, but also a thank you for just being so nice to me. She seems like a really good friend, and I can't remember the last time I felt that way about someone, you know?"

He bobbed his head. "Totally. Yeah, that would be great. I would love to meet her."

"Cool. She was only available on Friday this week. I

told her we had your family dinner but if there was any way we could reschedule it I would tell her."

"I'm sure we can reschedule. This sounds pretty important to you. If Friday is what works for her, we can make it work. I'll call my mom. Don't worry about it."

"Wow, thanks, babe. I really appreciate it. I hope you'll like her. She's really nice. I think she works in something with law, but I'm not totally sure what. We haven't really got into all those topics yet."

I saw him pause for just a moment, then resumed spreading shredded cheese onto the pizza. "Oh, that would be interesting. Does she work here in town?"

"No, I know she goes into Chicago for work. That's where her office is or something. But she can work from home? I don't know, it sounded complicated. I like to talk about tanning and makeup, you know!" I laughed a little, still playing the game and watching closely for a reaction.

He finished spreading the cheese around and this time turned to look at me. "Oh, that sounds like a nice setup."

"Yeah, definitely. But I'm sure you guys will have plenty to talk about, too. I feel kind of silly being this excited over a friend, you know? Like, I'm nearly thirty years old. Who cares if I have a new friend?"

His smile looked forced. "No, babe, it's awesome. You're never too old to make new friends. But I don't think you've mentioned her name yet."

"Oh, I haven't? It's Prue. Prue Doherty."

The look on his face said it all. I was going to fucking kill that bitch.

Chapter 30

PRUE

Harrison and I had a lunch date set up for the following day, Wednesday. Two days before I was to go into the home he shared with his wife, posing as her friend. I wondered if she had told him yet. Maybe she wasn't going to tell him and I was going to be a surprise guest on Friday. But no, that couldn't happen. I had to tell Harrison. I had to get out of having dinner. I had to do something.

I didn't hear from Harrison that day, and I was too afraid to text him myself. My stomach was about in knots. What if Nellie told him my name? What if he realized that I knew his wife and that I was still trying to see him? What if he realized what a horrible person I was? What if . . .

Pretty soon, I found my head over the toilet, vomiting up my meager breakfast I had forced down that morning. Of course this would happen to me. The one time in my life

—the one time!—I tried to be selfish and just go for something I wanted, this would be the case. Apparently married men were off limits. What was I saying? Of course they were off limits! How had I somehow convinced myself I was doing an okay thing getting involved with Harrison after I realized he was not only married, but married to someone who thought I was her friend?

Because I was falling in love with him. I was. He had me literally from first sight. Our first casual conversations while walking, I felt something for him. As I got to know him—not as a married man and not as Nellie's husband—I felt the connection between us. So maybe I wasn't doing the right thing after I realized who he really was, but I was already in too deep. If only I hadn't Googled him right away, I could have stayed blissfully unaware of his marriage and not have felt so damn bad. But he shouldn't have been the one to accept and to basically hide his wedding ring from me those first few times. He played me. And that wasn't fair.

I flushed the toilet and brushed my teeth, getting angrier by the minute. I was the one wronged here. Harrison led me on, not the other way around. And Nellie? She cheated on Harrison! Even after he put an amazing diamond ring on her finger, she couldn't keep her legs closed. She clearly wasn't a good person and didn't care about Harrison or their marriage. Maybe those two were meant for each other.

I looked in the mirror at my pale face and bloodshot eyes. When I saw Harrison tomorrow, I was going to give him an earful. How dare he lead me on? How dare he put my heart in this situation, when he knew about my past.

And Nellie? I hadn't figured her out yet, but I would. Yes, I would.

* * *

Are we still on for lunch?

I sent off the text message to Harrison that morning and felt my heart pounding against my ribs as I waited for his reply. I had an idea, but I somehow needed to get him here, to my apartment.

It was nearly thirty minutes later when the reply finally came through. Clemmie was snoring on my bed, clearly not feeling my anxiety.

We are.

Okay. Not a whole lot to go off of there.

Do you think you could pick me up? My car won't start this morning.

A total lie. But how else could I get him here?

My phone buzzed right away this time. *I'm not sure that's a great idea. We can reschedule.*

Crap. Now what? *I really wouldn't ask if it wasn't important. I think we need to talk. Soon.*

Well, that was true.

Another reply. *What's your address?*

A smile spread across my face. A gentleman was always so easy. Got him.

* * *

I got a text around noon that Harrison was there. I ignored it. He needed to come to my door. Another text. I started to sweat a little. I hoped he didn't leave. I didn't really think this totally through. One more text. I got up from my spot on the couch and started to walk toward the window, to see if he was still out there, when I heard footsteps outside my door, then a knock. I froze.

Taking a deep breath, I walked steadily over to the door, hoping beyond hope none of my neighbors happened to be walking by when I opened the door.

"Prue? Oh my God, what are you doing?" Harrison shouted when I opened the door, standing in front of him in nothing but sheer lingerie. He turned his head and avoided looking at my body.

"Come in. Please." I tried to say this seductively, but I knew this was all wrong. All wrong.

"Prue. What the hell are you doing?" he asked again, still not looking at me.

I tried to shove down the tears. "Please come in so I can shut the door. Please."

I saw him hesitate but step inside. I tried not to consider this a victory. But he was in my apartment. We were alone.

The moment the door closed, I launched myself at him. I shoved my face against his and kissed his lips. My hands roamed his firm chest as I reached down for his pants and tried to pull his untucked shirt out. His hands reached out to grab my wrists, but I shook them free and instead pulled off my skimpy top, which basically was see-through anyway. I shoved it down so both breasts were exposed, and then put his hands on them. It all happened so fast and was so fuzzy that I felt like I must be on some sort of drug. I couldn't believe I was doing this.

Harrison's hands cupped my breasts for just a

moment, just an achingly pleasurable moment, before he snatched them away. "Prue. Stop this! Stop!"

I had never heard Harrison yell. I looked up at his face, which was bright red. I looked down at my chest, my bare chest, and threw my arms over my exposed body. "I'm sorry," I shouted, before running to my room.

Clemmie looked at me as I entered the bedroom, where I had locked her in so she wouldn't interrupt my time with Harrison. She looked at me with knowing eyes, as the tears started to come. What had happened to me? Why did I just fling myself at a married man? Undress myself in front of a married man? I was so ashamed.

There was a knock on the bedroom door. "Prue? I think we need to talk."

After I got dressed, I told Harrison we could still go to lunch if he wanted to be in a more public place with me versus my apartment, but he said he would rather just talk here and now. I wondered if he didn't want to be seen with me in public now, but I felt too numb to really get into it. I would never forget that scene in my doorway. Stripping. Putting his hands on me. Getting rejected.

I walked out, and Harrison was sitting at the kitchen table. The only other spot to sit was the couch, so this made obvious sense. I took a seat across from him, wondering how this would start.

"Prue."

"Harrison."

"Do you know my wife?"

That was not what I expected first. I took a deep breath. "Yes. I know Nellie."

He leaned back in his seat and closed his eyes. "How?

Why? I don't . . . understand."

He looked so hurt. "Listen. I didn't know you were married when we first started talking. I didn't know Nellie was your wife when I first met her at her tanning salon. It took me a while to figure it out all out. But you're the one married here, Harrison. You shouldn't have agreed to meet me. You shouldn't have kept agreeing to meet me. We shouldn't have exchanged numbers or flirted over text or long lunches. I may be in the wrong here, but you are, too. *You* are the one who is married!"

I sat back in my seat and took a deep breath. That felt good to get off my chest.

Harrison looked stunned. "You're right. You're absolutely right about that. But why didn't you tell me you knew Nellie? That you were friends with her. She has such high praise for you. She really thought you had a good friendship going!"

"You know what? I really don't want to talk about me and Nellie right now. I first want to understand this, us." I waved a hand back and forth between us. "Why didn't you tell me right away you were married? Why did you lead me on like that? And even after you said you were, why did you keep seeing me? After what I told you about my ex, you still deceived me like that? Why would you do that?"

He looked down into his drink. "I don't have a good reason. I was being selfish. I admit it. And I'm sorry. I really am sorry, Prue. You don't deserve that. Especially you. My marriage was feeling—wrong. Not that Nellie was wrong, it just felt like something was off for a while there. It felt like we were growing apart and there wasn't any passion between us." I winced, and he noticed. "I'm sorry.

I'm just trying to tell the truth. And then all this baby talk. We—well, I guess you probably already know that story." I knew I looked ashamed when I nodded. "That was putting so much strain on things. And then all of sudden you were there, and pretty and friendly and seemed to take a real interest in me. You talked to me. You seemed to care about my job and my work and my clients and my day. It just felt good to finally be able to make a connection with someone when I felt I wasn't getting that in my marriage."

"What made you decide to tell me you were married?" I asked quietly.

"Nellie said she was going to go to the doctor to get checked out and if she was all good, we were going to start trying for a baby. And right around that time, we just started connecting again. It felt like the old days with us. And that's when I realized what I had been doing. And it wasn't fair to Nellie. To my marriage."

Ha. Like Nellie really considered that when she decided to screw that Calvin dude. "So what? You realized you actually did love your wife. Then why keep seeing me? I'll admit I didn't make the best judgement call when I continued to see you after I realized you were married, but why did you? If you were suddenly so happy with Nellie and going to try for a baby—why continue to string me along?"

"I don't know." He put his head in his hands. "I'm sorry, Prue. I'm so sorry. I'm a Class-A jackass, I know that. But then I had started to develop feelings for you, too, and even though I knew it was wrong, I didn't want to stop seeing you. I found myself looking forward to our dates, knowing I was in for a fun time with you and good conversation. And that was wrong. And I know it."

"It was wrong. I was really falling for you, Harrison," I said quietly.

"Why did you do . . . this?" He threw his hands up and kind of shook them around. I assumed he was asking about earlier, and I felt my face heat up.

"Can I plead temporary insanity?" I tried to crack a joke, but it fell flat. "I'm sorry. I know that wasn't fair to do. I just thought if you could see me as a woman, as more than just a casual lunch date or business acquaintance, that you would realize it was me you wanted. That is so unfair. To everybody. And myself." I could see that now. What an idiot I had been. I was never there for Harrison to choose. He had already chosen. His wife.

"I didn't realize how far along your feelings were. I don't think I was really thinking about anyone but myself," Harrison said, looking at his hands. My mind flashed to them on my breasts. That image, that feel, would be burned in my mind forever. "I'm not usually like that. I don't know what happened to me."

"Same here." We sat in silence for a while, both reflecting on our bad decisions.

"I've really made a mess of things." He looked miserable. "I never meant to hurt anyone. I got carried away. And now . . . I don't know how to handle things."

I felt myself crumble. I knew Harrison was a decent man. He really didn't mean to do this, to cause this horribly awkward situation. I had to take a piece of the blame, especially after the stunt I pulled tonight. So did he, for continuing to see me. But so did Nellie. I drew a breath. "It's not your fault, Harrison. I have to take some blame here. Even after I knew you were married, I tried to pursue you. And that's not okay. And for tonight . . . I really can't say I'm sorry enough. I'm embarrassed, I'm ashamed. And I'm just sorry. I'm sorry we're in the situation. Really, I am."

"I don't know how to tell Nellie this. She's going to be so upset," he said. "She doesn't deserve this. And we want to try for a baby. Well, we are trying for a baby. I'm so sorry," he rushed out when I felt my face collapse at hearing him confirm this. "But I've wanted to be a father for so long. We were in such a good place and now this . . . and she was so excited for you to come over and for me to meet you. She said we would probably have a lot in common and she was thrilled to have a real friend. Nellie doesn't make friends too easily, but maybe she told you that. She's had a difficult life and now I have to ruin this for her. I feel awful."

I nodded slowly. How dare Nellie make Harrison feel this way? Well, sure, she wasn't doing it directly right now, but I could bet Nellie would spin this situation to make her look like the good person. It seemed that had been what she was doing her whole life. But I couldn't let that happen. I couldn't let her get away with this. And I couldn't let Harrison fall into her trap. But what could I do?

The answer seemed obvious. Tell Harrison about Calvin. Nellie had cheated, right before they had gotten married. Had a full-blown affair, right under his nose, probably as he was helping plan (and pay) for their glamourous wedding day. So what we went on a few dates? She had sex with another man. She was clearly hiding something about all this baby stuff. He couldn't stay married to her. And I could give him a way out.

But it could look like I was going to tell him just to spite Nellie. I didn't want to come across as spiteful or that I just wanted to win in this situation. I had to handle this delicately. One wrong move and it all could come crashing down.

"Harrison," I said slowly, and waited for him to lift his head and look at me. "Can I be really honest with you right now?"

He nodded. "Of course. Please."

I took my time speaking, my game plan running through my head. "Even after I realized who Nellie was, it was more than just my feelings for you that somehow convinced me what I was doing wasn't totally wrong."

His eyebrows scrunched together. "I'm not following."

"Well, you see, Nellie has . . . told me a few things. About her. Personally. Once I realized you were her husband and what she had been doing . . . it was kind of easy not to feel as guilty anymore. It doesn't make it not wrong and I'm not trying to justify that, but, that's a part of it. And I just wanted you to know that."

He had gotten very still. "What do you mean? What was she doing?"

I took another breath, looking him right in the eyes. "Honestly? I don't feel comfortable saying it. I think it's a conversation you need to have with your wife. But you might want to ask her who Calvin is."

Chapter 31

NELLIE

"Who is he?" Harrison asked me quietly. It was Wednesday after work. Harrison had come home and said we needed to talk. So she had done it. My "friend," the first person I had actually let into my life in so many years, had turned out to be nothing but a fake. A despicable person who had used me to get close to my husband. I couldn't believe I had been duped in such a huge way. She had truly pulled one over on me.

I took a deep breath. "Who is Prue to you, Harrison?"

He winced and sat down hard on the couch. I was seated on the edge of the chair, my hands clasped together. I felt oddly calm. My marriage could very well be ending tonight, but I wasn't sweating or nauseous or anything else that I thought I might have been. I knew I had fucked up when it came to Calvin, but Harrison was no longer the perfect man I thought he was.

"I know I'm not perfect. By any means. But I don't understand how my new friend fits into your life. Who is Prue to you?" I repeated, watching him closely.

"I wasn't having an affair," he responded with, looking right at me. "And who is Calvin to you?"

I kept my voice calm. "I did mess up, Harrison. I did. And I'm truly sorry. I can't say that I can explain everything, but I can be honest with you and tell you why or what I was feeling. But first, I really have to know. How do you know Prue? How did you meet? I thought she was my friend." My voice caught on the last word, much to my horror. "Was this her plan all along?"

"I met her in the summer, when I would go jogging. She has a dog, and I would stop to pet Clementine—the dog. It started out as innocent chatter. One day she asked me to coffee. I never thought—I didn't know—you never seem interested in me. Or—you never used to. I was feeling lonely. And she seemed nice. And—I don't know. It just felt good to have someone interested in what I was talking about. My job. My day."

I nodded, encouraging him to go on, even though I had sudden sense of nausea.

"Nothing happened. We would meet for coffee or lunch and just talk. I told her I was married. But then we kept meeting and talking and I found I was really connecting with her. And things just started to spiral out of control. But I didn't sleep with her, Nellie. I promise you that."

My smile felt raw. "We're two very different people, you know that?"

He looked at me quizzically. "Why do you say that?"

I shrugged. "You had an emotional affair. I had a physical affair." I saw his face contort in pain as I said the deception aloud. "It was before we were married. I know that doesn't make it right, but I somehow convinced myself that it wasn't as bad. I freaked out. I was scared. I'm not good at commitment. I . . . there are things in my past that I've never shared, and I was afraid you would find out some day down the line and hate me and regret me, and I freaked out and yes, I slept with another man. I'm not proud of that. But I never strayed once we were married. Not once. I meant what I said when I took my vows. And I love you, Harrison. So much." My voice hitched and the tears started, but I kept going. "I'm not good at talking. About emotions. Letting people in. You're not good in the physical department. It's easier for you to talk than to show. It's easier for me to show than to talk. We each betrayed each other in the way we only know how."

"How?" His voice was a whisper. "How did we end up here? Is it all my fault?"

I stared at a spot on the wall. "It's not all your fault. You can't put this solely on you. Sometimes I felt like you thought I was petty or I couldn't keep up with your conversations, so I stopped caring. I kind of stopped caring that you didn't want to talk. When you started working more, I just let it be. I never bothered to find out what was really wrong." I took a deep breath, and looked at him. "When Calvin moved to town here, I was so paranoid that it had something to do with me and that he would try to ruin things for us again. I told him to stay away, that I didn't want anything to do with him. But it made me so scared that everything would fall apart. But, it's just a coincidence he's here. He's in a serious relationship and moved here for her. But I was still paranoid, so what do I do? Hell, I tried to turn to my new girlfriend to get advice from her. What a fucking joke that turned out to be, huh?" I laughed, and Harrison looked even more dismayed. "I'm so truly sorry for what I did. I shouldn't have cheated when we were engaged. I shouldn't have hid it from you all these years. I should have talked to you about how I was feeling. I know I broke your trust in me, and for that, I can't apologize enough. I love you, I love being married to you, and to know I let myself be careless with that, it infuriates me now. You didn't deserve this. And I'm sorry." Each word I spoke came from my heart. I meant everything I was saying to him.

"I don't know what to do from here," he said, sounding strangled. "I don't know if I can get over you sleeping with someone else. But I'm sorry I started seeing her. I was feeling such a distance from you. And all this baby stuff—I felt like you were never going to want kids and I felt confused and frustrated and lonely. I told myself as long as I didn't sleep with her, it wasn't really a big deal. But I didn't even think about the term emotional affair. But that's exactly what I was doing. How did I end up there?"

I had no idea how our story would end, or continue. How did we move past this? How could we both forgive each other?

"I know it might take some time, but I really hope we can find a resolution," I said. "But I also need to figure out Prue. She was clearly manipulating me to get closer to you. Why would someone do that?"

He shook his head. "And she seemed so nice, too. And she had a tough situation in her past. I would never have thought she was capable of something like this. It's shocking."

"Shocking. That's right." And I would not let her get away with it. "I'm assuming she's not coming over tonight as planned. But I might need to pay her a visit."

"Nellie." Harrison looked at me. "I'm sorry I made you feel lonely."

My heart skipped a beat. "I'm so sorry I made you feel lonely. You're my best friend. Honestly." Honestly. "I love you so much. And I'm so sorry."

I started crying then, real, ugly tears streaming down my face. We met each other halfway and were suddenly clinging to one another, our tears mixing together. I felt desperation as I hung on to my husband, not just to hold on to this life, but to really hold on to him. He hurt me, that was true. But I couldn't imagine not waking up to him every day. I couldn't imagine not hearing his voice, smelling his scent, hearing his laugh.

"I'll be better," I heard myself saying. "I know I can be. You mean everything to me."

"I love you, Nellie. So much. Please. Please don't hurt me again," he said, cupping my face. The pain on his face was cutting me open. It hurt so much to see his pain. I hated it. I hated this feeling. I hated what I had done to him.

"I won't. I promise. Please love me. Don't stop, okay? I'll always be here for you. Just me. No one else, okay? Please love me."

My life changed in a huge way that night. While I

didn't know what our future held, how our marriage would be repaired, I understood then that I was capable of loving someone. Of sharing all of me, of being vulnerable. My past could no longer define me. I was ready to move on from the demons that constantly haunted me. I was free.

Chapter 32

PRUE

Six Weeks Later

Saturday morning there was a knock on my door. Clem strolled over to the door and sniffed at it, then lifted her head back and let out a howl. I was in the kitchen scrambling eggs together and felt a few flashes of emotion —trepidation, fear, curiosity. Who could it be? Harrison?

I looked through the peephole and saw Nellie standing there. I jumped away from the door, as though it had burned me. Oh my God. Oh my God. What did I do? I couldn't let her in here. There had been silence from her and Harrison for over a month. I made sure I stayed away from places she might be. I did try texting him a few times, though I got no response, and frequented the restaurants I knew he liked, hoping to run into him. It was a sickness. But I was slowly trying to get over it. Over him. I had moments of weakness, though. My biggest low was when I showed up at his work last week. I shouldn't have given the receptionist my real name. I was politely but firmly asked to leave. I hadn't heard a word from Nellie this entire time. I thought it was a little odd, but I didn't actually know her. I didn't know how she would react in the situation. I should have known better, though. Of course she would show up. But what did she want? And why was she here, at my apartment? Now?

Clemmie kept barking, and I continued to stand frozen. Nellie knocked again, and I still didn't move. Suddenly, she spoke.

"I know you're in there, Prue. Let me give you a word of advice—don't contact Harrison again. Don't let me see you again. You betrayed the wrong person." Her voice gave me chills. It was low, menacing. Dangerous. She stared hard through the peephole, as if she could sense I was watching her. I started to sweat. "Friendly tip, doll. My husband isn't going anywhere. Certainly not to you. I don't want to know that you showed up to his work. I don't want to know you called him ten times in two hours. Whatever it was you thought you had, it's over. Completely over."

And then she turned and left. I immediately found my phone and dialed Harrison's number. If she was here that meant she wasn't with him. Maybe he would finally talk to me. It went to voicemail.

I threw it on the table and sank to the floor. Was I really going to get no answers? I thought I could handle losing Harrison, but I was kidding myself. I loved him. During the many conversations I'd had with my mom on this subject, she mentioned the word obsession. But I wasn't obsessed. I deserved this. I deserved a happy ending. I deserved Harrison. Nellie didn't.

I called again, desperate. This time, as though he could finally sense my desperation, he answered.

"Prue? You can't call me anymore. Stop texting me. You need to leave us alone." His voice sounded different, and I felt my heart break.

"Why, Harrison? Why? Why would you want to stay with her? You know who she really is now. She doesn't love you!"

His laugh was hollow. "You befriended Nellie to get closer to me and sift information from her. I don't know if I've ever met anyone as manipulative as you. It disgusts me that I thought you were a good person. You used Nellie, and you used me. You're despicable."

With that, the line went dead. I stared at the cell phone in shock. Oh my God. He never sounded like that toward me. It was truly over. Nellie had gotten to him, and she had won. And why should I be surprised? She was his wife. I had lost. Again. I lost with Deacon, and I lost with Harrison. I really thought it was my chance to win. Just this one time.

I curled up in a little ball right on the floor, feeling the pain radiate throughout my entire body. Why did I deserve this? I always tried to do the right thing, always. The one time I tried to be selfish, to go after what I wanted, and this is how it ended. Of course. I didn't deserve a nice guy like Harrison. Nice girls would always finish last. Always.

Clemmie came over and started to lick my face, then lay beside me. She seemed so concerned, so I reached out to pet her soft fur. "What do I do now, girl? What do I do?" I cried so hard my stomach started to hurt, but I couldn't get myself to stop. This was the lowest I had felt in a long time. The haze was somehow lifting. I had tried to take someone's husband. I had let a woman think I was her friend, just to get closer to her husband. I threw myself at a married man, tried to get him to be unfaithful. I was disgusting. How did I move on from this? I was so ashamed of myself.

I heard another knock on the door and froze once again. This time Clemmie didn't bark, she stayed by my side. At least my dog would always be loyal to me. Who was it now? Harrison? Nellie? My mom?

I slowly got up and tiptoed to the door. Peeking through the small peephole, I saw Nellie standing there once again. "I apparently didn't make myself clear the first time, Prue. You know, I tried to be the bigger person here. I didn't come after you like I wanted to. I didn't smear your name around town. I tried to be better than that. And you know why? In all our conversations, I found that I wanted to be you." Her laugh was hollow. "The good girl. Making the right decisions. Being unselfish. You made me want to be a better person, because I truly thought that's who you were. How ironic that you were just playing me for a fool the entire time." She paused. "Let me just say this. I might have made plenty of mistakes in my past, but that's not who I am now. I'm a better person currently, and that's what matters. It doesn't matter you've always been the good girl, because currently, you're the one that keeps fucking up. Our past doesn't define us. It's who we are now, and who we are striving to be, that makes us who we are. Save your poor girl sob story. You made these choices, you chose this path. And stay away from my husband. Don't call him again. And if you still find yourself wanting to call him, just keep this in mind."

She suddenly disappeared from my view, but I jumped back as an envelope slid underneath the crack of the door. She straightened, coming into my line of vision again. "I'll wait while you open it," she said, smug clear in her voice.

Were they suing me? For what? What could possibly be in the envelope?

I crouched down and picked it up, slowly tearing it open. It was obvious Nellie knew I was here, so why bother to pretend otherwise?

I took a picture out of the envelope. It was an ultrasound. Nellie and Harrison's name was printed at the top, and the black and white image stared back at me. They were pregnant.

"We should really be thanking you. If it wasn't for what you tried to pull, we might never have had the serious conversation we needed to have about our marriage and how much it means to both of us. We're going to be just fine, thanks to you, Prue. And now we have a baby to look forward to. Maybe we could name it after you?" The bitterness in her voice was clear. "I don't know why you did what you did, but it's over now. Harrison is my husband, and the father of my baby. Stay away from us. I won't tell you again."

I sank back down onto the floor and heard her footsteps fade away, hopefully for good this time. I threw the ultrasound picture across the room but it only fluttered a few feet in front of me, stopping photo-side up, taunting me.

Nellie's words vibrated through my body. The past doesn't define us. It's who we're striving to be. And what was I striving to be? Why had I thought just because I was a good person in the past that would give me a get out of jail free card for any bad decision I made in the future? Who thought that way? And more importantly, how did I fix what my life had become?

I would never be able to forget that humiliating moment with Harrison. Of throwing myself at a married man. Or allowing myself to become the spoiled, selfish woman I had become. When did the change begin? Why didn't I see it? I somehow convinced myself that all those moments in life, from Tina in fifth grade to Marley in middle school and Carli in college and now with Deacon and Brandi, trying to be the better person and still getting the short end of the stick, had now made me feel like I deserved something. I deserved to catch a break.

But in that frame of mind, I had lost track of what all was good in my life. My relationship with my mom. A friendship with Linds. A career I worked hard to obtain. The beauty of being able to say I loved my job. My health. Clemmie. Having a purpose each day. I lost track of all the good in my life. And that had changed me. Had changed me into someone I didn't want to be.

Clemmie once again nosed my cheek, and I dropped my head into her soft fur.

"What happened to me, girl?" I whispered into her fur. "And why do you still love me?"

She calmly licked my face, and I felt something inside me stir. The loyalty of a dog is a beautiful thing, and I felt like in that moment Clemmie was telling me to get it together. She needed me, relied on me, and loved me. I couldn't just keep falling apart like this. Clemmie needed me, my mom needed me, and I needed me. I had let myself go to a dark place these last few months, but really, that was nothing. I could right my wrongs. I could get back on the right track. Because that's what I did. I was the good girl. I made the right decisions. I couldn't let the Harrison and Nellie situation define me. And I wouldn't. I vowed right then, on the floor with Clem, to make a change. And that change would start with moving out of this small town. It was time for a fresh start.

NELLIE

My hands were shaking as I left Prue's apartment. I couldn't believe she had the audacity to call Harrison after what I had told her. I knew showing her the ultrasound picture should finally get her away from us. But how dare she?

I climbed in my vehicle and let my head drop back against the seat. I couldn't believe how these last few months had played out. I thought I had befriended a likeable, easy-going woman. Turns out she was just waiting to backstab me and steal my husband. I realized that my seemingly perfect husband was human. And that I had to give my all to my marriage, because I wanted it. And not just the perfect life that seemed to come with being Mrs. Harrison Hawthorne. But because I loved my life. Without even realizing it, while being too stubborn to admit what was clearly in front of me, by letting myself think I would always let my past define me, I didn't realize the terrific life I had built for myself. I had told Harrison the entire truth about me, my mom, my past, even how we met. How my mom was a drug addict and prostitute, and that I found her dead body in our yard one cold winter morning. Apparently, she overdosed while out and whomever she was with dumped her body outside our trailer for her daughter to find. But no matter what horrific story I told Harrison, he continued to hold my hand through the words, the stories, my past. I was terrified that even after all the talking we had, all the times Harrison told me no matter what I had to tell him he would never stop loving me, that when I told him I had duped him when we first met, that he would up and leave me.

But he hadn't. Over the course of four days, my entire sordid story slowly spilled out. I cried so many tears I was surprised I could even function. I let the girls at the salon know I needed a few personal days and Kerri took charge, telling me not worry about anything and she would personally make sure everything ran smoothly in my absence. I was so happy I remembered to buy her a new Michael Kors purse for her Christmas bonus because she continued to save my ass. I stayed up late at night, not being able to sleep, staring at my husband lying next to me and hoping beyond all hope that he wouldn't leave me. Realizing how true my love was for him, no matter how our relationship might have started out.

It was entirely liberating to tell Harrison. To show my true colors, to be so vulnerable to this man, and to have him accept me. All of me, flaws, scars, and past demons. I think Harrison and I both realized over these past few weeks how deep our love was for one another, and while it was slightly terrifying, it was also the best feeling I could have ever experienced. We were brutally honest with one another, to the point of fights occurring and ill words being spoken, but we did it all to better ourselves and our marriage. We loved one another more coming out of those black days, and it was truly, entirely worth it.

And now, we were given the greatest gift—a baby. I had to think it was a sign, a sign that everything was meant to be. Calvin, Prue, our honesty and fights. We had made it through some of the hardest things a marriage can endure, and we came out on the other side. And now, we were able to start a family. It solidified to me that everything must have happened for a reason. While I wished we never had to go through anything remotely similar again, I was okay now with the past. It brought us to the present, and while I reached down and touched my still-flat stomach, I smiled. What defines us? I thought for so long I would always be defined by my past, and I realized now how wrong that was. It was just as I told Prue through her apartment door. What defines us is who we are currently striving to be. And I worked on being not just a better wife, but a better person, every single day. I would no longer think I wasn't good enough for happiness. I would embrace that happiness and never feel the need to look back.

THE END

If you enjoyed *DEFINING HER…*

Get lost in *A Questionable Friendship*, the best-selling title from Samantha March with a shocking ending….

A QUESTIONABLE FRIENDSHIP

Prologue

September

"Brynne? It's time for you."

I moved my head just inches to the left, indicating I had heard my mother. I stared into the mirror, taking in my black dress with a hint of bubble skirt, the string of pearls around my neck, and my red lips. Portland was always going on about the importance of lipstick, though I hardly ever wore any.

"Brynne? Everyone is waiting." I finally turned away from my reflection, meeting my mother's eyes. She squeezed my hand and slipped the index card with my speech on it into my sweaty palm. "You'll be just fine, darling. You can do it."

I nodded, feeling my brown bob graze my neck and then brush away. I walked out of the small room with my mom, entering the large area where everyone awaited my speech. I took my place, my hand shaking as I looked at the index card. I looked out over the sea of people, everyone from our small town there supporting Portland. I looked at my best friend next, taking in her shiny blonde hair, her smooth skin that never seemed to find a blemish or a sunburn, even when we stayed on the beach for hours. Her white dress didn't clash with her fair skin or light hair, it just made her look like she was glowing.

I cleared my throat. "Portland Dolish is my best friend." I looked over at her once more, tears filling my eyes. I paused before I could continue, and wrapped up just after a few minutes of speaking. I had agonized on my speech just nights before, reading and re-reading and making changes until my husband Aaron told me it was perfect. I hoped he was right. Portland deserved this day to be perfect.

About the Author

Samantha March is an author, editor, publisher, blogger, and all around book lover. She runs the popular book/women's lifestyle blog ChickLitPlus, which keeps her bookshelf stocked with the latest reads and up to date on all things beauty, fashion and fitness. In 2011 she launched her independent publishing company Marching Ink and has five published novels – Destined to Fail, The Green Ticket, A Questionable Friendship, Up To I Do and Defining Her, and one holiday novella, The Christmas Surprise. You can also find her on Youtube sharing beauty reviews and creating makeup tutorials. When she isn't reading, writing, or vlogging, you can find her cheering for the Green Bay Packers and Chicago Cubs. Samantha lives in Iowa with her husband and Vizsla puppy.

Acknowledgments

As I start to write these acknowledgements, I already have tears in my eyes. I started writing this story while going through an incredibly hard time in my personal life, and Nellie and Prue became my escape. I found a comfort in my characters like I really never have before, and watching their stories unfold became like a therapy for me. And now here we are. This book is ready for the world, and I came out of writing it in such a better place than before the first word was written. And I have so many people to thank for that.

First, to the amazing community of friends and supporters I have found through the virtual world. Social media is not for everyone and can surely have its downside, but for me, I have formed so many special friendships and bonds with people all over the world, and I will always be grateful for that. It brings me an indescribable joy every day to talk to and connect with so many friends about books, makeup, fitness, and snapchat filters. To my family, who continues to show me what unconditional love is. From my husband to my mother to my in-laws, I'm insanely lucky to have the support system I do. And I can never forget about my lovely Grams watching from above, and who helped me fall in love with the written word. World Series Champs, Grams, can you believe it? Go Cubs Go. Thank you to Kayla Paine for being my beta reader, and to Chrissy at EFC Services for proofreading and Karan Eleni for the amazing cover. And thank you to my readers. You fuel me to create more stories and you continue to let me pursue my passion. For that I will be forever grateful. Thank you.

Made in the USA
Monee, IL
15 October 2022

15947252R00167